Praise for
Antoinette Truglio Martin

Another excellent read. Great historical fiction should take the reader back in time and let the story unfold as if the reader is there, worrying about every challenge and sharing the joy of every success. It should be a vivid representation of the time, allowing the reader to learn just by enjoying the story. The characters should be as real as any normally flawed good or bad person might be.

As a homeschool father, I would put **The Dreams of Singers and Sluggers** *into the hands of my children and teens. Just like the first book in the Becoming America's Stories series,* The Heart of Bakers and Artists, *the story depicts what it was like living through the time of the story while developing a great love of reading. The imagery of the story can so easily settle into the readers' DNA and become almost as real as any other memory.*

Brava, Antoinette. You did all this and much more. Brava!
Gary A Wilson, Author

Loved **The Dreams of Singers and Sluggers!** *I cheered and applauded.*
Kathleen Miller Collins, Registered Nurse

In **The Dreams Sluggers and Singers**, *nine-year-old Lily Taglia has a secret. The child of Italian immigrants, she's discovered a paradise in the lower east side tenements of 1911; a place where she can sing her heart out and her little sister Gigi can play in safety, the Henry Street Settlement. When the opportunity to perform with the chorus in public presents itself, Lily has to find a way to get her parents' permission and risks losing the dream of her lifetime.*

As in its predecessor, **The Heart of Bakers and Artists**, *Antoinette Truglio Martin uses rich description and well-researched* *details to bring the dangers and challenges of Lily's world on the lower east side to life. It is a story of hardships, hopes and growing up.*

Jacqueline Goodwin, MFA Author

What do you sacrifice to follow your dream? That's the challenge Lily, a young girl growing up in New York's Lower East Side faces in Antoinette Truglio Martin's book, **The Dreams of Singers and Sluggers**. *The story is set in 1911, where being a child of a poor immigrant family makes it difficult to have a dream because it interferes with daily survival and her parents' expectations.*

Today's young readers are offered the opportunity to step back in time and observe how difficult it was to grow up in an era that was common for young children to attend to school, while also having jobs and helping with family responsibilities. Despite a grueling schedule, Lily, and other children, have dreams and hopes, and they struggle to achieve them, despite the odds.

The author also introduces readers to the traditions and cultures of those who settle in New York's melting pot. In addition, we learn how important social programs, such as the Henry Street Settlement, helped families in need during this era.

But this book is not only about life's hardships. Readers can enjoy a Highlanders baseball game and sing along with a familiar tune. So, grab some popcorn and settle in for an enjoyable reading experience.

Pat Black-Gould PhD Clinical Psychologist

" I recently read the book **The Dreams of Singers and Sluggers** *and absolutely fell in love with it. It took me back to another time in history and transported me into the lives of immigrant families and their struggles, joys, heartaches of finding their place in America. Antoinette did a beautiful job weaving the stories together. You will fall in love with Lily and her family, as well as friends and neighbors and the lives they live. You will find yourself dreaming with them, rooting for them, feeling every emotion they feel"*

-Kirstin Troyer, Blogger

THE DREAMS OF SINGERS AND SLUGGERS

Becoming America's Stories

ANTOINETTE TRUGLIO MARTIN

In memory of my mother-in-law, Helga Martin, a dedicated nurse, and to all the patient and caring nurses that crossed my path.

CONTENTS

INTRODUCTION

Writing historical fiction involves collecting data and facts while letting imagination run loose. Once again, I fell into rabbit holes, devouring volumes of historical material. The first two decades of the 20th century established many foundations that created the American history we know today. History does not happen at one moment or date and was not the consequence of one person's actions. Previous events, policies, and fate set up the remembered time and place and inspired a few to stand out from the crowd.

I culled through dozens of facts, scenarios and the family stories. So much intrigue! It tempted me to put in everything. For the sake of craft and clarity, I banished pages and chapters into a file labeled "For Another Time", and tightened the tale, making the plot move and keeping the characters true to their spirit.

New York City's Lower East Side in 1911 was a fascinating time of reformation and progress that affected newly arrived immigrants and generations of Americans. I was drawn to the mission of the early public health nurses who ventured into the bowels of the Lower East Side neighborhoods, bringing care and hope to the poor. The tenements were a beehive of disease, corruption, and despair. Most of the nurses' wards were immigrants trying to establish their American dream.

Public Health nursing was born from Settlement houses that popped up in Manhattan and neighboring boroughs. The nurses ventured into the tenement neighborhoods, befriended the people, treated what they could in the comfort and affordability of their homes, and offered support and access to improve hygiene and children's health. The beginnings of community services and social work emerged.

One Settlement stood out. The dynamic Lillian Wald founded the Henry Street Settlement. Miss Wald came from an affluent German-Jewish family in Rochester, New York. Although she could have easily slipped into a life of comfort and privilege, she insisted upon becoming a nurse and serving the poor of the Lower East Side. She believed that education and health services would lift the poor from poverty and, thereby, inspire generations of loyal citizens.

There was an abundance of stories Lillian Wald conveyed in her speeches and books. She saw beyond the squalor and instituted a series of social and health programs to benefit the communities. The Henry Street Settlement became the meeting house for organizations. Labor unions, women's suffrage groups and the budding NAACP sat around the dining room table discussing solutions. There were classes for young mothers, sponsored dance and music performances, and a safe play space for children. Miss Wald and her dedicated staff petitioned school boards to hire nurses, offer lunch programs and create welcoming public education environments for all children. They marched for peace and were powerful voices on the long road to women's suffrage.

The Henry Street Settlement was located less than a mile from my story's Mott Street 1911 location (making it a viable premise). It still stands and continues today as a vibrant community center. I am grateful for the guidance of Katie Vogel, who took me on a private tour through the house. If you are in lower Manhattan, the Henry Street Settlement is a must see.

There is no evidence of my great grandmother or her daughters having a direct story to the public health nurses or the Henry Street Settlement. From the oral stories my grandmother told, it seems they relied on homemade salves and medicines and stregas with mysterious chants and brews. However, they most likely benefited from the outcomes Lillian Wald pioneered. One aunt recalled getting milk in school. The labor reforms in the factories and holding the right to vote directly affected their young lives.

Baseball was another compelling rabbit hole. Baseball was the American game and became the universal language shared by all tongues and social classes. It brought everyone into a conversation. Before radio, the newspapers were the one media outlet to convey story after story of the game, the players, and the state of the fields. Baseball sold newspapers and became the source of good news that was read out loud with the family.

New York had three teams in 1911—the New York Giants, the Brooklyn Trolley Dodgers, and the Highlanders. The newspapers occasionally dubbed the Highlander players Yankees or Yanks because they were in the American league. The Highlanders played in the dumpy Hilltop Park and struggled to keep the momentum of fans coming to the park. That year, the Highlanders hosted the Giants for half the season since the Polo Grounds had a fire and underwent a rebuild. By 1912, the Highlanders folded, sold, and eventually re-branded as the New York Yankees.

No matter which team was rooted for or scorned, baseball quickly fed into tenements and onto the streets. Stickball was a favored and affordable means to play the game in the alleys. Boys loosely organized themselves, collected cardboard and garbage can covers for bases, and "borrowed" their mother's broomsticks. Although girls were rarely invited to play, I imagine many stopped to watch, jeer, and cheer.

My grandmothers and aunts were not as die-hard of baseball fans as their fathers, uncles, and husbands, but they had opinions about trades and called umpires "bums" on the television. In my family, the Brooklyn Dodgers were never forgiven for leaving Ebbets Field and moving to the sunny west coast. The Yankees and, later on, the Mets filled the void, but the lament endures.

The Dreams of Singers and Sluggers picks up where **The Heart of Bakers and Artists** left off. The history of how children played, forged friendships, and survived in the Lower East Side tenement neighborhoods inspired wonderful stories that resonate in today's playgrounds, classrooms, and family tables. Perhaps you will recognize yours.

CHAPTER 1
DON'T RUN!

Friday afternoon, May 5, 1911

LILY SCURRIED through the crowded school hallway. She could not wait for Nelly, her best friend. Once outside, she ran down Baxter Street dodging women carrying food for their suppers, peddlers hawking the last of their wares, and store keepers sweeping the sidewalk in front of their doors. Her long quick strides sailed over an overturned can of garbage. Carts, patient horses, and motor cars with blaring horns congested the busy street. Lily could hear Mama's warnings in her mind.

"Don't run in the streets. Watch out for a car. Don't run behind a horse," she'd say.

Lily shook Mama's loud voice from her head. She could run faster in the street. It was a warm spring day, perfect for running.

Lily gripped her grey shawl and sped to an opening in the crowded Little Italy street. She was eager to get home, but first, she had to pick up her Daily Bread at Goldberg's bakery. Margaret, her eldest sister, would be there and have news about Mama and the baby. Lily hoped that this time there was a baby brother.

Just as Lily headed for the Hester Street corner, the oysterman stepped into her path, holding a sharp knife in his gloved hand and handing out an opened shellfish to a cluster of customers.

"Watch where ya' goin, kid," he shouted. "I coulda' stabbed ya'!" Beratings in Italian and English from the customers followed.

Without an apology, Lily continued her race to the bakery. Margaret would have scolded her for being so clumsy and rude, but Lily had no time to be polite. She had to hurry. She planned to hold the baby before Mama sent her outside with little sister, Gigi, to buy a potato or greens. Later, she could meet with Nelly, at the stoop and play patsy before Papa came home. Lily wondered if Papa would have his way and give this baby an Americana name, rather than a Sicilian name like her and her three sisters. The girls went by American nicknames, even though Mama preferred their Old World names.

Earlier that morning, Lily rose from the bedroll on the floor she shared with her three sisters in the front room. It was still dark in the small room that served as a sitting and dining room and the four sisters' bedroom. Like every morning, Lily quickly dressed without waking Gigi, still dreaming and sucking her thumb. She carefully walked around the bedroll, feeling for Papa's big chair next to the window, then the table and two chairs pushed against the wall.

Unlike every morning, Mama still wore her nightgown as she paced around the small kitchen table, holding her enormous belly. Lily's big sisters, Margaret and Betta, folded rags and sheets. A large pot of water boiled on the stove.

"Keep the windows closed. No drafts for the baby," instructed Mama, panting.

Margaret grabbed Lily and quickly weaved her copper-red

hair into one long braid. "Go to the Goldberg's and start the Daily Bread. You will have to do all the mixing and kneading by yourself. I probably won't see you at noon. Tell Mr. Goldberg I will be in later today to count the register and tabs."

"Mrs. Goldberg will be so excited to finally see the baby," said Lily. "Mama, you must see all the booties she knitted— not one match!"

Margaret gave Lily's braid a tug. "Please tell Mrs. Goldberg to wait until tomorrow. There's a lot to do today."

"This baby will come quickly, like all of my babies," said Mama, "We will have plenty of time to get everything done today."

Papa sipped the last of his coffee, picked up his lunch pail, and donned his gray cap. "I'm making deliveries on Long Island today, but I will be home before dark."

Mama gripped the edge of the table and blew out a loud sigh. "We'll be here with a new mouth to feed. Perhaps a boy this time."

Papa kissed the top of Mama's head. She had already brushed and pulled her thick black hair into a round bun at the nape of her neck.

"I'll be home to help as soon as I pick up my Daily Bread, Mama," said Lily. "I promise."

Mama held Lily's face in her long, calloused hands and kissed the child's forehead. Lily's bright blue eyes met Mama's deep brown eyes. At age nine, almost ten, Lily stood as tall as her strong Mama. She would grow long and lanky, like Betta, but hoped she would be as strong and determined as Mama.

"Go to school, my songbird," said Mama, "Everything will be alright."

∿

When Lily finally burst into the bakery, she saw everything was not alright. Mr. Goldberg, not Mrs. Goldberg, stood behind the glass counter. "Where is Margaret? Where is Mrs. Goldberg?" asked Lily.

Mr. Goldberg raised his right bushy eyebrow and smiled. "Good afternoon, Lily. I do well this day, thank you. And how you do?"

Lily smiled back. Mr. Goldberg had a friendly way about him. He calmed short-tempered customers and Margaret's sour moods. The sinewy man was gentle with his wife, who was often distracted with dreams of ballet or swallowed in memories of terrors from their Old World life. He never raised his voice, only a right or left eyebrow.

"I'm sorry, Mr. Goldberg," said Lily, "I thought Margaret would be here to tell me about the new baby. Is Mrs. Goldberg with my mama?"

Mr. Goldberg handed Lily a round loaf of golden bread. It was warm. Lily knew it was her Daily Bread she mixed, kneaded and shaped because there was a letter L etched on the top.

"I don't have three cents," said Lily. "Margaret has the money."

"I put on tab," said Mr. Goldberg. This time, he raised his left eyebrow. "Mrs. Goldberg shop for supper. Too nervous waiting. Tell her babies take time. She decide to cook. Make big soup."

"Didn't Margaret come to count the recites and money?" asked Lily.

"No," said Mr. Goldberg, "Babies take time."

CHAPTER 2
RUN, LILY, RUN!

LILY RAN to 125 Mott Street with her Daily Bread tucked under her arm. She raced up the stoop stairs into the dark hallway. Mama was going to have to remind Mr. Russo, the janitor, to fix the light in the stairwell again. Lily smelled sweat, pee and old fish. The tenement always smelled like old fish on Friday afternoons, but today, she did not let the reek slow her down. She stretched her legs two steps up at a time to her home on the fourth floor.

Lily heard muffled agony increase at each floor landing. It did not sound like Mama. Mama never cried out in pain. Perhaps another woman was having a baby or maybe someone was hurt and being stitched. Last month, young Mrs. Czneck (who was only three years older than Margaret) cut her hand on the pickle man's cart. She carried her baby on her hip with the other hand and trailed blood up to her second-floor home. Mama washed the wound with vinegar and sewed seven stitches in the shrieking woman's palm. Lily and Gigi heard her screams from the fourth floor.

By the time Lily reached the fourth floor, she knew the commotion was coming from her door. The three other apartments on the floor were shut tight, but the toilet closet door was wide open, sending out its foul odors. Lily closed the narrow toilet door. All four families shared one toilet. Mama usually took it upon herself to clean it each day, but it did not look or smell like anyone bothered today.

Lily opened her door and walked into a steamy kitchen. A pot furiously boiled on the stove and Margaret, leaning over the deep sink, hand-squeezed water from a sheet and rags. Thirteen-year-old Margaret wore Mama's white apron and had her sleeves rolled above her elbows. Loose curly tendrils of dark hair framed her sharp face.

"Good. You are finally home," she said.

A guttural howl came through Mama's bedroom door. Lily stood frozen in place. She had never heard such a painful cry.

Margaret plunked the wet sheet and rags in a basket.

"Something is wrong," said Margaret, lifting the basket to the table. "I got the Strega, Signore Bocchino, to help." She wiped the hair from her eyes and took a deep breath.

"Stoke the stove. Water has to keep boiling. Pay attention and don't make a mess with the ashes. Then take the laundry to the roof and hang them to dry. And make Gigi stop crying. She's under the couch."

Lily placed her Daily Bread next to the basket and Margaret slipped into the bedroom. Lily swept the ash, added more coal nuggets to the stove bin, then wiped her black hands on her pinafore. Her hands were still caked in damp ash. She washed away the dirt before touching anything else. Lily decided her hands were too clean to take the ash bucket down to the garbage. Margaret could do it later.

Lily coaxed Gigi and Principessa, Gigi's rag doll, out from under the couch.

"Come on, Gigi, you can be the big sister helper."

Hollers and screams seeped out of the bedroom. Gigi clutched Principessa, stuck her thumb in her mouth, and shook her head.

"No big sister," she said, lisping through her thumb-filled mouth, "Me baby sister."

Gigi pulled at Lily's skirt as they stumbled up the stairs to the fifth floor and then into the rooftop's narrow stairwell. Lily tripped and toppled the basket.

"Help me pick up the laundry, Gigi," said Lily, but the little girl sucked her thumb and sobbed. The child wailed when Lily asked her to hold the clothespins and she continued to cry while Lily draped the sheet and rags on a line.

When they returned to their apartment, a fresh pot of clean water gently bubbled. Twelve-year-old Betta sat on the cot next to the stove. She pressed a rag against her forehead. Although frequently plagued with a blinding headache or a hacking cough, Betta always kept her red hair combed and braided, and her blouses and skirts neat and clean. But this afternoon, Betta's mussed hair and soiled clothes betrayed the toil in Mama's bedroom.

"Margaret said I could take a break," explained Betta.

"When will the baby come?" asked Lily. Gigi, still clinging to Lily's skirt and Principessa, crunched her eyes shut upon hearing sharp yelps from the bedroom.

"Margaret fetched Signora Bocchino late this morning. Mama didn't want to spend the money on the Strega. She thought she could do this by herself like she did with all of her babies. Since Margaret was staying home from school to help, we didn't need Signora Bocchino. After hours of horrible pain, we had no choice. But Signora is no help, and we already paid her with the money from Mama's coffee can. She insisted. The witch stares with those mismatched eyes; one blue, the other yellow."

Betta had a way of rambling and running out of breath without answering a question. Lily was trying to stay balanced with Gigi clutching and sobbing at her side.

"When will the baby come?" interrupted Lily.

Betta looked up from her rag. The sparkle in her blue eyes

dimmed. "We thought the Strega could help. Mama never had a baby like this before. I never saw Mama so scared."

Margaret slipped out of the bedroom door. Her brown eyes darted about the steamy room.

"We need you, Betta, come back." Betta sprung to her feet, wringing the rag in her long hands. Although exactly a year younger than Margaret, Betta stood a half head taller in a delicate frame. In contrast, Margaret's demanding voice, and neck and arm muscles revealed strength in her short, lean body, just like Mama.

"You'll have to hold Mama's arms down to keep her from swatting at the Strega," said Margaret. Lily noticed Mama's white apron was smeared with blood and grime.

Mama is going to be mad about getting those stains out of her apron, and the coal soot from my pinafore, thought Lily.

Before closing the door, Margaret spied the coal bucket filled with ash. "Take that to the garbage," she told Lily.

It had been hours since Betta and Margaret returned to the bedroom.

"Don't cry, Gigi. The baby is almost here."

"Mama. Want Mama," moaned Gigi.

Lily wiped away a tear before it fell on Gigi's head.

"Let's sing a song. What do you want to sing?" suggested Lily.

A long shrill shivered up Lily's spine, causing Gigi to push deeper into Lily's side. Any hope of a song vanished.

Papa burst through the front door. He threw the newspaper on the table. Gigi jumped off the couch and flew into his arms. He picked the small child up and stared at the bedroom door. Lily scrambled off the couch and leaned against Papa's side. How she wished she was little, like Gigi, so Papa could hold her, too. But Lily was nine years old, almost ten, too big to sit on his lap or carried in the safety of his embrace.

"How long has she been like this?" asked Papa.

"Most of the day," said Lily. "They had to get Signora Bocchino. I found Gigi under the couch."

Papa paced around the small kitchen table, his gray cap still perched on his head, covering his thick mane of copper-red hair. Gigi held fast around his neck, her twin brown braids hanging over Papa's thick arms. Papa knitted his forehead in worry, making the scar over his right eye throb purple.

Betta slipped through the bedroom door, clutching soiled sheets. A volley of angry rants followed her into the kitchen.

"Oh, Papa, you're home!" exclaimed Betta. Sweat trailed down her face, and her collar and underarms were damp from the heat and exertion.

"Signora Bocchino wants to get the priest," continued Betta. "She said the baby is stuck and probably dead, and Mama is so weak." Her voice caught on a sob.

Lily grabbed the edge of the table. Gigi hiked her legs and arms tighter around Papa. The big man stood stoned-face. His blue eyes brimmed with tears.

"What can we do, Papa?" asked Betta.

Finally, Papa pulled a large pot from the ceiling hook and threw it into the sink. The rattle jolted Lily and Betta. Still holding onto Gigi, Papa dug his hand into his pants pocket and pulled out a fistful of bills.

He turned to Lily. "Run, Lily, Run to the house on Henry Street. Tell them we need a nurse right away."

"Yes, Papa, a nurse!" cried Betta.

"Get a nurse," continued Papa. "Pay a cab to bring you and the nurse back home."

"Signora Bocchino will not like this," said Betta. A relieved smile crept on her face.

"Run, Lily. Run fast!" repeated Papa.

CHAPTER 3
NURSES AND HANDSHAKES

LILY RACED down the stairs and jumped from the stoop to the sidewalk. She leapt over a boy shooting a marble on the sidewalk, and weaved around people, carts, horses, and cars on Hester Street. She knew a shortcut through Seward Park. Her long legs pumped hard while her hand gripped the money. All she could hear were Mama's screams and Papa telling her to run, run fast.

Lily scurried around the big house on Henry Street and rapped on the kitchen door where she had delivered bread, rolls, and Mrs. Goldberg's Knot Surprises on Saturdays and Sundays. She was still gasping for breath when the door opened and a short, plump woman with dark hair piled in a top bun stood in the entryway.

"Lily darlin'! Whatcha' you doin' here, lass?"

Lily heaved for breath as the woman pulled the girl into the vast kitchen. "Miss Patty, please. My mama, my mama is in a terrible way. The baby is stuck and—"

"Say no more, lass," interrupted Patty. "I'll fetch Miss Wald."

Lily stood in the middle of the large kitchen. Warm aromas of simmering stews, blanched vegetables, and sweet pies teased Lily. A long loaf of bread from Goldberg's bakery sat in a basket covered with a white linen. Lily's stomach yelped at her hunger pangs.

Just as Lily's breath returned to a normal pace, a tall woman dressed in a smart shirtwaist and gray skirt walked into the kitchen. Patty scurried behind.

"I am Lillian Wald—head nurse at the Henry Street Settlement," said the woman, holding out a thick hand. Lily had never shaken the hand of a grownup before. She delicately took the woman's hand and bowed a shallow curtsey.

Lillian Wald chuckled. "My, quite the young lady. You can simply shake my hand, woman to woman."

"Yes, ma'am," said Lily, giving a slight shake to the firm hand. "My name is Lily Taglia. Mama's baby is stuck. Signora Bocchino says the baby is dead and Mama is weak. She wants to get the priest." Lily caught a frightened sob in her voice.

Miss Wald turned to Patty. "Mrs. O'Shea, please have Violet ready a bag. She can tend to the poor woman while I run the meeting."

Patty quickly scurried away.

"Come with me, Lily Taglia," said Miss Wald.

Lily followed the woman through the back room into the main part of the house. They passed beautifully framed portraits on the wallpaper walls and a tall clock with a swinging pendulum ticking away the minutes. Lily peeked into the front parlor, where a gathering of men and women stood and sat around a long table. She spied an upright piano tucked in the corner.

"Mr. Horowitz," called Miss Wald. A young man excused himself from the small group. Mr. Horowitz, a stocky man dressed in a dark jacket, had to lift his chin up to meet Miss Wald's eyes.

"Yes, Miss Wald," said Mr. Horowitz.

"Mr. Horowitz, this is Lily Taglia. Her mother is having a

very difficult labor. Would you be so kind to drive Violet and Lily to her home on, hmm?" Miss Wald turned to Lily. "Lily, dear, do you know your address?"

Lily would normally feel insulted that someone thought she did not know her address. She would have snapped back and say that of course she knew her address. But today, Lily did not have the time to defend her knowledge and honor.

"125 Mott Street ma'am," replied Lily, holding out the bills from her pocket. "Papa gave me money for a cab."

"125 Mott Street," repeated Miss Wald, ignoring Lily's outstretched hand.

"Certainly. I'll bring the car around right away," said Mr. Horowitz. He pulled his cap from his jacket pocket and left through the front door just as a young woman dashed down the staircase. She was just as tall as Lillian Wald and wore a gray ankle-length skirt and blouse with a white collar and cuffs. A dark gray ascot was tied in a loose bow around the collar. Patty stepped behind her carrying a black bag and gray brim hat.

"I am ready," said the woman. "This must be Lily. Patty tells me of your sweet voice from the weekend bakery deliveries." She held out her long hand to Lily. Handshaking must be the way nurses say hello, like men, thought Lily. Lily held her hand and gave the woman a firm shake.

"My name is Violet Forsythe," said the woman, taking the bag and hat from Patty. "Let's take care of your dear mother and baby."

~

The black bag sat between Lily and Miss Forsythe. Lily felt a great weight lift from her chest. This lady in gray, who shakes hands like a man, was going to take care of Mama and everything will be fine, as it should be.

"Papa gave me money to pay for a cab," whispered Lily to Miss Forsythe.

"Nonsense," said Miss Forsythe, "Mr. Horowitz enjoys a spirited drive, don't you Mr. Horowitz?"

"That's right, Miss Violet," said Mr. Horowitz from the front seat. "Nothing more exciting than a brisk drive through the Lower East Side on a fine Friday night." He turned to face Lily and winked. "We'll be there in a flash."

Suddenly, Lily thought of Connie, Margaret's best friend who liked to wink at friends. She was killed in the Triangle Shirtwaist fire just two months ago. Connie baked Daily Bread with Margaret every morning. When Lily joined Margaret to learn how to bake Daily Bread, Connie often had a chummy wink. Everyone liked Connie since she was friendly and chatty, not like sour Margaret.

Lily squeezed back the memory. The motor car swerved to the left and just as quickly swerved to the right, barely avoiding a newsie boy carrying the evening papers.

"Hey, watch where ya' goin', lunatic!" shouted the boy.

"Best to keep your eyes on the road, Mr. Horowitz, lest we arrive in one piece," said Miss Forsythe. She calmly sat back as though they were driving on a quiet country road.

"Sure thing, Miss Violet," said Mr. Horowitz, bringing his attention back to the street.

CHAPTER 4
FINDING GOOD NEWS

LILY RACED up the four flights of stairs carrying Miss Forsythe's black bag. The nurse climbed close behind. Lily held the doorknob and noticed how quiet and still everything felt. She thought perhaps the baby got unstuck—or maybe—

"I'm back! I'm back with the nurse!" exclaimed Lily, bursting through the door.

Papa stood in front of the stove. Two big pots boiled clouds of steam. Margaret sat on the cot, cradling Gigi's curled body.

Miss Forsythe stepped in, hung her hat and cape on the pegs, and rolled her sleeves past her elbows. "Is there clean water in one of those pots?"

Papa pointed to the pot on the right side.

"Ladle some of that water into a deep bowl. Gather clean rags," said Miss Forsythe.

"Signora Bocchino left to get the priest," blurted Margaret.

"Well, we'll see about that," said Miss Forsythe. She grabbed her bag and let herself into the bedroom.

Betta soon slipped out of the room, "She wants the bowl of water, Papa."

Papa handed a chipped bowl to Betta. Mama mixed macaroni and gnocchi dough in that bowl.

"She wants you to help, Margaret," said Betta.

Margaret lay whimpering Gigi on the cot and followed Betta into the bedroom.

Papa scooped Gigi into his arms. The little girl looked as limp as Principessa.

"Come to the front room, Lily," said Papa, "Find good news to read to us."

Lily sat at the table in the front room and opened the newspaper. She could barely make out the headlines. Muffled moans travel through each room.

"Find any good news, Songbird?" asked Papa. He sat in his big chair, holding Gigi close, looking out to the darkness of the long day's end. He dubbed Lily *Songbird* because she frequently burst out a song or hummed a tune.

"I'm looking, Papa," said Lily. The only good news Lily wanted to see was **Mama Births a Sturdy Baby Boy and Cooks Supper for the Family**. She turned the newspaper page and pointed to a headline. "It says the New York Highlanders traded two outfielders for a hot-dog batter named Curly Crisp. He played in the Wichita Jobbers minor league and has a 324 average. Is that good news, Papa?"

Papa sniffed. "That is good news. That boy can hit a rock with a stick clear out of a park. Them Yankee Highlanders sure do need a slugger."

"Where is Wichita?" asked Lily.

Papa shrugged. "Not sure. America is a big country."

Betta rushed out of the bedroom and into the front room.

"Papa, Papa!" gasped Betta, "The nurse said the baby's heart is still beating. She said to go to the saloon and bring back a pint of dark beer."

Papa quickly stood up and spilled Gigi in a chair next to Lily. He grabbed his cap and was out the door before Betta could remind him to hurry.

Betta mixed a spoonful of sugar with clean hot water into Mama's coffee cup. She stirred, breathing in the warm sweetness, and leaned on the wall between the kitchen and front room.

"The nurse said the dark beer will ease Mama's pain a bit, and it's good for Mama's milk," said Betta smiling reassuringly. "It's going to be okay, Lily. Mama and the baby will be just fine, Gigi. You'll see."

"Pomise?" lisped Gigi through the thumb stuck in her mouth.

Betta's smile disappeared. She retreated to the bedroom.

"Come on Gigi," said Lily, "Let's find some more good news to read to Papa when he gets back."

Gigi nodded her tangled head and leaned on Lily. She wiped a puddle of drool on Lily's sleeve.

"Big sisters don't suck their thumbs, Gigi," said Lily, "You are four years old, almost five, and too big to act like a baby."

Gigi popped her thumb out of her mouth. "I show baby how to suck a thumb."

CHAPTER 5
A LIVING PRINCIPESSA

LILY COULD HEAR Papa pound up the stairs. His long legs and heavy feet climbed fast and steady. Lily opened the door with Gigi, thumb in her mouth, tugging at Lily's skirt. Papa burst in, holding out a pint can.

"Dark beer," he huffed. "Bring it to Mama."

"Don't you want to bring it to Mama? See Mama?" asked Lily. While Papa was gone, short bursts of screams followed by gentle murmurs leaked through the bedroom door. Lily did not want to see her strong Mama in pain, or her big sisters in distress, or the confident nurse defeated. The air suddenly felt too thick to breathe. Lily wanted to be a crybaby, like Gigi. Didn't she do enough as a nine, almost ten-year-old girl? She carried wet sheets to the roof, minded Gigi, ran to the Henry Street Settlement and brought back the nurse.

Before Lily could say she was too scared to go into the bedroom, the rooms fell silent. Moans and murmurs ceased. Echoes from the hallway slipped from the walls. Even the boiling water stopped gurgling. Papa, Gigi, and Lily held their breath as they looked toward the bedroom door.

Just when Lily thought the worst had happened, a loud wail, that could only come from a new life, rang out.

"The baby! The baby is here!" cried Lily. "Gigi, do you hear our new baby?"

Gigi held Lily's hands with a tighter grip.

Papa stood stone-faced against the door, holding onto the handle of the pint can. His blue eyes welled with tears. The sounds of the rooms and tenement hallway fell back into place. Scurried whispers peeped through the bedroom door. Lily and Gigi leaned into Papa's side. Lily wasn't sure who was holding up who as they waited for the door to open.

Finally, Margaret slipped out the door. Her face was streaked with sweat and red lines rimmed her dark eyes. She held a small bundle.

"Look here," she said, "We have a brand new sister."

Lily and Gigi left Papa's side to peer at the little face. The baby's eyes were closed, and her little lips were puckered in a tiny pink bow. Her rosy cheeks almost looked painted. Light wisps of yellow and auburn hairs fell on her forehead. She looked like a baby doll that sat in Christopoulos' General Store at Christmas time.

"Miss Forsythe said she is perfect. She had a hard day, but she is strong," reported Margaret. Her voice was soft and sweet.

Papa cleared his throat. "Mama? How is your Mama?"

"She is weak, but Miss Forsythe says she will get strong again," said Margaret, "We will all have to pitch in and help." She stared at Gigi.

Gigi stuck her thumb in her mouth, avoiding Margaret's glare.

"Can I hold her?" asked Lily.

Margaret nodded to the cot for Lily to sit on. Lily pulled Gigi up next to her and Margaret gently placed the bundle in Lily's waiting arms. The baby felt so light. She sighed a content breath. Gigi buried her head into Lily's shoulder.

"Look, Gigi, she is a living Principessa," said Lily. Gigi ignored the request.

Papa put the pint can on the small table and stepped closer for a better look. He gently took the baby from Lily. Gigi lay down behind Lily, thumb still in place.

"She looks like you, Lily, when you were born," said Papa, "Pretty and pink."

"Sorry, it wasn't a boy, Papa," said Margaret. "Mama thinks you may be disappointed."

"A little girl can never disappoint me," said Papa.

Papa returned the baby to Lily. He wiped his eyes and nose with his jacket sleeve, then turned to Margaret. "Bring the dark beer to your mama."

"Miss Forsythe said you should bring it in," said Margaret. "Don't forget a clean glass."

CHAPTER 6
NOT A FAIRY TALE

Friday afternoon, May 12, 1911

LILY KEPT in step with Margaret's quick stride. The day was bright and smelled almost clean, even though the scent of fish and horse manure mingled in the air.

Lily hummed the *Star Spangled Banner* Mr. Crandall, the music teacher, had taught that afternoon.

Mr. Crandall liked to change the music arrangements to make the same old songs sound fresh. He frequently chose one or two students to step to the front and sing a refrain or punctuate a line. This time, he chose Lily, (a fourth-year student) to sing a part in the national anthem at the Moving Up ceremony next month.

"Lily, your voice is loud and clear. I want to feel those rockets glare red," said Mr. Crandall, wiping his prominent forehead.

Lily loved to sing in school and would not be shy about stepping in front of the chorus and belting out her part.

ANTOINETTE TRUGLIO MARTIN

"Make sure you know all the words by heart. I will see you in two weeks," said Mr. Crandall. A two-week gap was better than the usual once-a-month music class.

Lily couldn't wait to tell Mrs. Goldberg. She and Mrs. Goldberg shared an artist's heart. Lily loved to sing, and Mrs. Goldberg loved to dance. The baker's wife was once a ballerina in the Russian Ballet (that life was a secret Lily swore to God not to tell to anyone, not even to Nelly). Lily and Mrs. Goldberg created and performed steps to songs Lily made up in the bakery basement. Although Margaret rolled her eyes and Mr. Goldberg gently reminded his wife that there was work to be done, the joy brightened the bakery basement. Even the Goldbergs' simple nephew, Aaron, who could not speak, read, or write, perked up from his labor. He was a strong worker who shoveled coal into Dragon, the bakery's hot oven, and carried sacks of flour and sugar onto pallets. When Lily sang and Mrs. Goldberg twirled, Aaron clapped and showed his wide smile that reminded Lily of a jack-o'-lantern pumpkin.

～

"Pick up your Daily Bread, then go straight home, Lily," ordered Margaret, "Get the laundry off the roof and keep Gigi out of Mama's way."

"Didn't you hear me, Margaret," said Lily, "Mr. Crandall said—"

"I heard you," said Margaret, weaving around candle cart customers. "It's grand the music teacher chose you to sing, but right now singing the Star Spangled Banner is not as important as chores."

"You are so bossy, Margaret," said Lily.

"I have to be bossy! You behave like a little kid who only thinks about playing and showing off. You make me crazy!" said Margaret.

24

Margaret was so difficult to talk to. Finally, they reached the bakery. Lily bumped into the door, but Margaret held it closed. Lily knew a lecture was coming.

"Listen to me," snapped Margaret. "You are so clumsy and selfish. The world does not revolve around you singing. The baby frets all day and night, Mama is not well, Betta is barely any help, Gigi constantly whines and cries, and Papa comes home expecting supper and peace. And to make matters worse, Betta read Mama the letter from Sicily, so now Mama is sadder."

∼

When a letter from Sicily arrived in the Taglia mailbox a few days ago, Mama couldn't wait for Margaret and Lily to come home. Mama usually waited so that all the girls could laugh and comment about Zia Teresa's gossip. Lily never met Zia Teresa or seen the little town Mama grew up in, but felt she knew every person and place. Mama never learned to read and write like her younger sister, so Margaret or Betta read the letters aloud.

Betta had hoped the letter may cheer Mama, so she read it aloud before Margaret and Lily returned home. The news was terrible. Zia Teresa wrote that their mother died from an outbreak of cholera. Several neighbors, including Mama's best friend's three children, and the parish priest had also perished. Mama retreated to her bed and remained in the dark with her tears and regrets. Among all of Mama's hopes, she longed to see her family one more time.

∼

"I'm not selfish, Margaret," said Lily, trying to open the bakery door. "I know Mama is very sad—somber like Aunt

Em in the Wonderful Wizard of Oz Betta read to us. Remember?"

Margaret rolled her eyes. "This is not a fairy tale! This is real life."

"I know," said Lily, growing impatient, "but I do everything! I go on errands for Mama, wash the diapers, fold laundry, mind Gigi, do school work, and hold the baby all the time. Now, I bake Daily Bread every day and all you do is go to school and study, You work at the bakery all the time to avoid coming home."

Margaret's lips tightened in an angry line. Luckily, a customer, who was leaving the bakery, tried to push the door open. Margaret quickly changed her angry face into a friendly smile. "Good afternoon, Mrs. Zimmerman."

"Good afternoon, Margaret," said the round woman holding a long loaf of braided challah bread. "Thank you for door. Ah, sisters, yes?"

Margaret and Lily nodded to the old woman. Mrs. Zimmerman liked to come in later in the afternoon when Mr. and Mrs. Goldberg had time to gossip. Mrs. Zimmerman lived alone in a tiny room on Hester Street. Their conversations mixed with English and Yiddish and always ended in hearty laughter.

"Cherish. Once had three sisters and two brothers. Lost to pogrom—the Jewish massacres in Russia." Mrs. Zimmerman waddled through the doorway. "Cherish. Sisters best friend forever."

Lily did not believe Margaret would ever be her best friend, but she politely nodded to Mrs. Zimmerman. Just as Margaret was about to close the door and give Lily another piece of her mind, Big John and Donny slid through the door.

"Thanks," said Big John, "It's good to see these independent gals are learning some manners, eh Donny?" Margaret growled low, losing the moment to scold Lily.

Big John and Donny put three cents on the glass counter

for their Daily Bread. Unlike Lily's loaf, the boys' breads were lumpy and heavy. They were careless in mixing and kneading, no matter how many times Margaret taught them.

Each day, Lily and other kids mixed, kneaded and shaped a loaf of bread for their family. They arrived at the bakery basement before school to mix the dough and returned at lunchtime to knead and shape. Later in the afternoon, the bread was baked and was ready for the children to pick up after school. They paid three cents a loaf instead of five, saving the families much-needed pennies each day.

Margaret was the best bread baker, even better than Mr. Goldberg (who was not really a baker, but that was another secret Lily vowed to keep). Since Lily could reach the baking table, Margaret now supervised the Daily Bread kids and helped Mr. Goldberg with the books. Margaret was a whiz with numbers. She was also a wiz at spelling, geography, sewing, embroidery—everything.

Although a year younger than her eighth-year classmates, Margaret won the eighth-grade math award and had the highest grades in her class. Big John, who was in Margaret's class, was jealous that a girl was smarter than him. Just a few months ago, he called Margaret terrible names and tried to hurt her. But Margaret socked him in the nose and almost broke her hand. To save Big John's honor, Margaret made up a fib that explained his bloody nose and her swollen hand. Big John and Donny became friends with Margaret and the girls — not best friends, just good enough friends. Even so, Big John couldn't help his naughty retorts about girls, and Donny always agreed with his crooked smile.

Mita Cohen, the newest Daily Bread baker and Margaret and Big John's classmate, counted out the three pennies onto the bakery glass counter. Her younger brother, Joshua, stood close to his sister's side. Joshua, Lily's classmate, was a small thin boy who spoke with a nervous stammer. He did not bake Daily Bread with his sister. Not only was he too short for the baking table, Joshua spent most lunch hours painstakingly writing on the blackboard in the classroom, "I will not tongue-tie words", or "I will write with my right hand."

"Hello, Margaret. Hello, Lily," greeted Mita, passing her Daily Bread to Joshua. Joshua hefted the bread and nodded to the Taglia sisters with a shy smile.

"How did your Daily Bread come out today?" asked Margaret.

"Very well, thank you," replied Mita. Mita stood eye to eye with Margaret. Her wiry black hair stuck out of her two braids. Her eyes were darker and her nose appeared longer than Margaret's. Unlike Margaret, Mita's smile softened her harsh looks.

Mita shooed Joshua behind her back so that Margaret could not get a good look at her bread. "My bubby said yesterday's Daily Bread was perfect. She dipped it in chicken soup last night, isn't that right Joshua?" Joshua nodded.

"Brava! Brava!" clapped Mrs. Goldberg.

Lily smiled. Mrs. Goldberg always had kind words for Mita, even though Mita's bread came out heavier and lumpier than the boys'. The baker's wife had a magical way to encourage without humiliating. Margaret frequently complained it was painful to watch Mita waste the flour to bake such poor bread.

"Mita will learn. Need time," Mrs. Goldberg told Margaret. Kindness was part of Mrs. Goldberg's magic.

Mrs. Goldberg's headscarf lay bunched on her neck, revealing a halo of golden hair around her head and fair face. Lily thought Mrs. Goldberg was the most beautiful woman in the whole world, and certainly the most graceful being that she was once a real ballerina. She was tall and lean with a fine chisel nose and green eyes that danced. When she was happy, her long hands fluttered as she spoke punctuating words, and her cheeks glittered from an overuse of sugar and (Lily believed) magic. But when Mrs. Goldberg remembered the terror that took her far from her home and the ballet, her eyes dimmed and face darkened. Mr. Goldberg, who had heroically saved Mrs. Goldberg in Russia, fretted as he tried to coax her back to the bakery. Several times Lily sang the melodies of her favorite ballet music. Since there were no words, Lily made up sweet lyrics or filled in with "la-la-las". The songs helped Mrs. Goldberg dig out of her melancholy. "Go home, Lily," said Margaret, making her way behind the counter. "Tell Mama I will bring home whitefish and potatoes."

Lily sighed, tucking her Daily Bread under her arm. "I always have to do everything," she mumbled.

CHAPTER 7
BASEBALL AT THE BAKERY

A YOUNG COUPLE glided into the bakery. The man wore a brown tweed suit with a thin black tie tucked into a tweed vest. A felt fedora covered his blond hair. The women wore a long black skirt and a smart white blouse with a delicate flower embroidery pattern on the collar. Her light brown hair was set in a low chignon bun and covered with a light brown cloche hat decorated with a bow on the side. It was Miss Smith, Lily's third-year teacher! Miss Smith had a soft voice and smiled at all of her students. She never slapped rulers on desks or hit students on the knuckles with a stick. Miss Smith was especially nice to Joshua Cohen. She never made Joshua write punishment sentences on the blackboard.

"Come along, Jane," said the young man, "We will have a cup of coffee with a treat before catching the trolley to the ballpark."

"A quick cup of coffee, Jack," said Miss Smith, "I can't wait to see my first ballgame."

"Hello Miss Smith," said Lily with a shallow curtsy.

"Why Lily Taglia! Is this the bakery you and your sister bake Daily Bread?" Miss Smith remembered everything about her students. "We heard it is a sweet cafe, now."

Mr. and Mrs. Goldberg decided to expand the bakery business. Mr. Goldberg built a few sturdy tables and chairs and set them in the shop for customers to sit and enjoy coffee or tea and a Knot Surprise—Mrs. Goldberg specialty. Margaret's bookkeeping confirmed business thrived and Mrs. Goldberg loved to chat with people.

"Sit. Sit by window," said Mrs. Goldberg, directing the pair to a small table, "Such pretty couple. Look, Simon, pretty couple come to cafe bakery!"

Mr. Goldberg looked up from the tabs and arched his right eyebrow. "Such honor," he said smiling.

Miss Smith blushed. The man, called Jack, said to Mrs. Goldberg, "Two cups of coffee and a Knot Surprise to share."

"Such a hurry? Sit. Enjoy," said Mrs. Goldberg.

"We are off to see the Highlanders play at Hilltop Park," said Miss Smith. "They are playing the New York Giants on the home field. So exciting!"

"Oh, must hurry," said Mrs. Goldberg with a chuckle. "A date to ball game!"

"Yanks need win," said Mr. Goldberg, arching his left bushy eyebrow this time. Lily wondered how he could individually move each eyebrow.

"'Dey got a new slugger, Curly Crisp," said Donny, "He got some swing."

"That's right," said Jack, "but the big news is that he is a kid from the Lower East Side. I'm writing a story about him."

"Mr. Reynolds is a newspaperman for the New York Sun," said Miss Smith proudly. "He reports on all the sports, but I love baseball best."

"You have to go home, Lily," reminded Margaret.

"Tell Mama, my good friend, I visit soon," said Mrs. Goldberg to Lily. The sugar on her cheeks glittered.

Lily re-tucked her Daily Bread under her arm and turned to Miss Smith and Mr. Reynolds. "Goodbye Miss Smith. I hope the Highlanders win."

Miss Smith smiled at Lily. "Thank you, Lily, dear. I understand your mother recently had a baby."

"Yes, a baby girl," said Lily. "Papa is not disappointed. He's happy that she is strong."

"That is good news," said Miss Smith.

"We named her Violet for the nurse who helped birth her," said Lily.

"A nurse?" asked Miss Smith.

"Yes, ma'am," said Lily, "Mama had a terrible time. Signora Bocchino left to get the priest, but Papa told me to run and bring back a nurse."

"Oh my," gasped Miss Smith.

"I ran all the way to the Henry Street Settlement to get a nurse," said Lily, "Miss Forsythe came and saved Mama and the baby."

Miss Smith turned to her friend. "The nurses at Henry Street are angels, Jack. They go into the tenements and provide needed medical care." Mr. Reynolds nodded his approval as Miss Smith turned back to Lily.

"I am so glad all is well," said Miss Smith. "Violet is a pretty name. It sounds American."

Margaret pulled Lily to the door and hissed, "Go home to Mama, Lily!"

"Okay, Okay! You don't have to be so bossy."

CHAPTER 8

BETTA ON THE STOOP

LILY WALKED HOME STEAMED over Margaret's pushy tone. Mama had been tired all week since Violet's birth. Margaret took over and bossed everyone, especially Lily. Lily had to do everything.

Betta sat on the front stoop clapping and chanting to Gigi's one-foot hopping count.

⬜Five!⬜announced Betta, ⬜That's the best so far.⬜

Gigi spotted Lily walking down Mott Street. ⬜Lily home! Lily home!⬜she cried, ⬜Come play.⬜

Lily ignored Gigi's plea. She was surprised to see Betta outside on the front stoop, wrapped in a spruce green shawl. Although Lily and Betta share the same copper-red hair shade and crystal blue eyes as Papa, Betta's beauty excelled beyond Lily's. Betta's hair shined in the bright daylight, her blue eyes sparkled clear, and her pale skin had a rosy glow that was not from a fever. Betta, who was always plagued with an ailment, rarely attempted the four ⬜ights down to Mott Street in the afternoons. Most of her fresh air came from an opened window in the front room.

⬜Betta, you are downstairs!⬜said Lily.

❏Miss Forsythe said I am responsible to improve my health and future. I must exercise my lungs so I can get strong. She told me to bring Gigi outside so we can both get some exercise.❏

❏How is Mama❏❏

❏Miss Forsythe is with her now. Little Violet fusses so, and Mama is exhausted. The caring for such a tiny baby never ends.❏

Violet cried all the time. Lily, Margaret, and Betta took turns rocking and carrying the baby through their three-room home. Papa also held Violet when Mama tried to catch up on her sewing homework for the sweatshop. Every day diapers and small dressing gowns were washed and hung to dry over the stove or on the roof if it was a bright day. Water constantly boiled on the stovetop. To add to the havoc, Gigi behaved like a wounded kitten. She whined, hid under the couch or behind Papa's chair, and sucked her thumb.

The worst part was seeing Mama so ❏uiet. She did not order Lily to stop singing silly tunes at the top of her lungs, making Gigi dance and Betta clap. She did not bicker with Margaret. When Papa came home, she did not pepper him with complaints about the terrible neighbors, the butcher's spoiled meat, the broken toilet in the hallway. Instead, Mama stared out the window and barely looked at the baby in her arms. Her hair stuck out of a careless bun and her apron remained stained. She constantly wiped tears from her dark eyes. She ignored Margaret's barbed comments. Lily missed Mama slapping her hand on the kitchen table, rattling cups, and demanding obedience. Even when Mrs. Murphy knocked on the door complaining about the noise, Mama did not argue or send the neighbor away with a *malocchio* curse.

Miss Forsythe opened the front door and stepped around Betta.

❏Lily, dear! Good, you are here,❏ she said. She handed

Lily a piece of paper, "Take this note to the milk station. The depot is on the corner of Broome and Mott Street. Bring back two cans of evaporated milk and a quart of pasteurized milk."

"How is Mama?" asked Lily.

"She needs fortification. She's still weak and feeling low." Miss Forsyth explained that because Mama was so tired, Violet was not getting enough milk. The baby needed evaporated milk to supplement her diet. Violet would have to learn to drink from a bottle.

"I don't have money for the milk," said Lily.

"Use the voucher," said Miss Forsythe, "The Settlement has special funds to supply needs for the community."

Miss Forsythe turned to Betta. "I want you to go back upstairs, dear. Go slowly so as not to strain yourself. Check on the bottles and nipples boiling in the pot. Take care not to burn yourself."

"But," squeaked Betta.

"No buts. We are a team. All of us have a job to do. Your job is to go upstairs by yourself." She turned to Lily. "Lily's job is to get to the milking station. Take Gigi with you."

Miss Forsythe bent down to Gigi. Gigi stuck her thumb in her mouth and tucked herself behind Lily. "And your job, little sister, is to mind your big sister." She gently pulled the thumb from Gigi's mouth. "Now dear, how can Lily hold your hand with that thumb stuck in your mouth?"

Gigi sneered, grabbed Lily with her wet hand, and put her left thumb in her mouth. Miss Forsythe stood up and adjusted her gray hat and cape. Lily thought Miss Forsythe must be a bossy big sister, like Margaret. Unlike Margaret, she did not shout or say that anyone made her crazy.

Miss Forsythe came to see Mama and Violet every day since the baby was born a week ago. At first, Papa balked, believing he would have to pay the nurse money he did not have. Miss Forsythe explained the city paid the visiting nurses.

Also, funds from good people called *philanthropists* helped support the Henry Street Settlement's missions. There was no charge for the health services and the other programs for the people of the Lower East Side.

Lily expected Mama to quarrel about the intrusion. Mama would have roared about the conceit of this young woman who did not have a husband and children, telling her how to feed her baby, and keeping her home clean. Mama was the cleanest person in the whole tenement, probably all of Mott Street. But that was the real Mama. This somber Mama was not real Mama.

Be sure your mother drinks a full glass of milk tonight. Divide the rest of the quart between each of you girls, including Margaret. She may think she is grown-up, but she is still a growing girl. Lily giggled.

Remind your mother to feed the baby two ounces of evaporated milk. If it does not satisfy Violet's hunger, she can feed the baby another ounce.

Tony Sbrozzi, the boy who lived on the fifth floor flat with his papa and big brother, Joe, came out of the street crowd to the stoop. Thin and gangly, he tipped his hat to Miss Forsythe and Betta. Tony was Betta's age and seemed to be sweet on Lily's pretty sister. He liked to visit and talk to Betta about the books they read. Betta dismissed the attention, saying he was more interested in Mama's cooking and being part of the family. After all, he called Mama and Papa his zia and zio endearing terms for aunt and uncle.

Afternoon ladies, said Tony.

Hello Tony, said Miss Forsythe, Perhaps you can help Betta with the baby bottles boiling in the large pot while the rest of us get on our way.

Gladly, said Tony, reaching for Betta's hand.

Betta can climb the steps on her own. Isn't that right, dear said Miss Forsythe.

"Yes ma'am," said Betta, "I do feel strong today."

"On your way to the milking station," said Miss Forsythe to Lily and Gigi.

Lily passed her Daily Bread to Tony. Gigi noisily sucked her left thumb.

CHAPTER 9
A TAG-A-LONG LITTLE SISTER

Sunday, May 21, 1911

LILY RACED to the Most Precious Blood church. She spent too much time chatting with Mrs. Goldberg and had to race to Mass. Her sisters were already seated. Lily skidded to the pew, genuflected, and slid next to Margaret just before the procession of altar boys and the priest marched up the aisle. A trail of incense followed them. Betta handed Lily her black rosaries with a relieved smile.

Mama was not strong enough for the walk to church with baby Violet, yet. The baby was happier with the evaporated milk supplementing her feedings. She did not cry all the time —only some of the time. When calm, Violet watched her sisters with a serious expression. She only turned her mouth up in a toothless smile for Papa and Betta's kisses. Miss Forsythe said that Violet was gaining weight and behaving like a healthy newborn.

Somber Mama, however, appeared small and pale. Her eyes, circled in dark rings, sunk deep into her head. Mama had not barked orders or scolded any of her daughters in the three weeks since Violet's birth. She barely ate and only drank a glass of milk when Papa slapped his hand on the table and shouted, "Cesca, you must get well. Your daughters need you." Last night he hissed at her, saying he needed her.

Gigi was also a worry. The little girl spent most of the day sitting on the floor next to the big chair, sucking her thumb. Principessa lay under the couch, unloved.

Lily settled into her seat and unburdened her worries to the Madonna. She prayed that her real Mama return soon and be the mother she and her sisters knew before Violet was born.

After Mass, the girls followed the crowd out into the bright spring day. Lily squinted at the sunshine.

"Such a lovely day," exclaimed Betta, stepping down the church steps without Margaret or Lily helping her along. She was getting stronger. Betta lifted her shawl from her head, revealing her shining tresses neatly combed and braided. At the end of her perfectly even braid, she had tied a merry yellow bow. Gigi had two matching green ribbon bows for each of her long brown braids. Before heading to the bakery that morning, Lily hastily combed her hair with her fingers and braided a long lumpy rope. She tied it off with a string of yarn.

Gigi held Lily's hand while sucking her thumb at the foot of the church steps.

"Will you be able to get home with Gigi by yourself, Betta?" asked Margaret. "I saved enough allowance to buy a white ribbon from the milliner. I need something to brighten my Moving Up dress."`

"I am feeling well," said Betta, "The daily outings have strengthened me. But Margaret, won't it be hard to get a white ribbon that doesn't show the dullness of the muslin?"

"I know," said Margaret. "I tried soaking the material in diluted bleach, but it is still dim."

"Does it have to be a white ribbon?" asked Lily. "Why not

get a color? Pink is pretty. Buy a pink ribbon." To Lily's surprise, Margaret and Betta did not balk at the suggestion.

"Hmm, maybe," said Margaret, "Hurry to the bakery, Lily. There is a big delivery of rolls and Knot Surprises for the Henry Street Settlement, today. Donny will go with you."

"Gigi, you go home with Betta," said Lily, trying to shake off Gigi's left hand.

"No!" said Gigi, gripping Lily harder.

"You can't come with me. You will slow me down."

"No!" repeated Gigi. She popped out her thumb from her mouth and held both of her hands to Lily's arm. "I don't wanna go home. No Mama. No baby." Gigi stamped her feet on the church steps.

Margaret sighed. "I have to go across Canal Street. It is too far for Gigi. Bring her to the bakery, then take her home before the delivery."

"I don't want a tag-along little sister with me," complained Lily.

Margaret smiled. "I know. Little sisters have a way of making you crazy. Don't let go of her hand."

As Margaret and Betta walked away, Lily looked down at Gigi. Gigi's big brown eyes looked up at Lily.

"I am not holding your slimy hands," said Lily. "Keep your thumb out of your mouth."

Gigi wiped her hands on her dress, then re-grabbed Lily's with her right hand and stuck her left thumb in her mouth.

"You're not a baby anymore," said Lily. Gigi stared ahead, sucking on her thumb harder. "Stubborn, like our real mama." Lily let out an irritated huff. "Let's go. And don't make me crazy."

CHAPTER 10
WET THUMBS

L ILY LED Gigi around the noise and crowds of people and peddler carts. Although it was Sunday, the neighborhood bustled with people getting through their busy day.

Mrs. Goldberg thrilled at the sight of Gigi climbing down the basement steps.

"Simon, look who come. Little Gigi!"

Mrs. Goldberg took the child's hands, not minding the wet left thumb, and danced in a circle. Gigi smiled for the first time in days.

"Ach! Too small for baking table," said Mr. Goldberg, arching his right eyebrow. "But check, my Anca. Soon new Daily Bread baker."

"Come, *maliya*, my sweetness," said Mrs. Goldberg, "We see big girl you are."

Gigi pulled her hand from Mrs. Goldberg. "No!" shouted Gigi, "I'm baby Gigi." Her voice smacked against the basement wall.

Donny, Big John, Mr. Goldberg stopped their work. Aaron put aside his shovel and peeked from behind Dragon. Mrs. Goldberg's smile faded.

"Poor child. Miss to be Mama's baby. Ach, Mama love you. Mama love grown up baby."

Gigi stuck her thumb back in her mouth and retreated to Lily's skirt.

"I'm sorry, Mrs. Goldberg," said Lily. "She is jealous of the new baby."

Mrs. Goldberg stood next to Lily and looked down at Gigi. Her cheeks glittered with sugar.

"Understand," said Mrs. Goldberg, "Sweet little girl. We dance another day. Yes? Friend? Yes!" She pulled a fat Knot Surprise from her apron pocket and offered it to Gigi.

"Say thank you," said Lily, nudging Gigi.

"Grazie," mumbled Gigi, and snatched the treat.

Lily finished kneading and shaping her daily bread dough quickly. She carved an L on the top and placed the raw loaf on the warming shelf. Lily showed her sister the scratched marking on the stairwell wall that led up to the bakery shop. With her back against the wall, Lily stood straight and tall. She placed her hand on top of her head and held it to the wall as she turned around.

"See, Gigi, I am at just the right height to bake Daily Bread. I started when I was just a smidge too short, but Margaret needed me to help her, so Mr. Goldberg let me use the small chair to stand on so I could reach. I don't need it so much anymore"

Gigi stuck her thumb in her mouth.

"One day you will be tall enough to reach the baking table," added Lily.

Gigi scrunched her face in an angry frown, like real Mama. "Basta!" she hissed.

Upstairs in the bakery shop, sweet warmth surrounded Lily's nose. Mrs. Goldberg finished packing baskets of round loaves and another basket of Knot Surprises to deliver to the Henry Street Settlement with Donny.

"Let's go," said Donny, grabbing a basket. "I'm in a hurry."

"I have to bring my sister home first," said Lily.

"We don't have time for 'dat," said Donny from the side of his mouth. "I'm playin' stickball with 'da fellas."

"But I told Betta I would bring Gigi home," said Lily.

"Bring her with us," said Donny. He leaned over to Gigi, "Ya' don't wanna go home and be stuck with a baby all afternoon, do ya'?" Donny's half-smiling face made Gigi giggle.

Two smiles in one day, thought Lily.

"I visit Mama. My friend," said Mrs. Goldberg. "I bring my friend coffee. Café?"

Lily took the Knot Surprise basket. She gave Gigi's dry hand a shake. "Just don't make me crazy."

Donny laughed. "Ya' sound like Margaret."

CHAPTER 11
A POWERFUL VOICE

GIGI KEPT up with the quick pace. They took the shortcut through Seward Park and down an alley. Donny waved to the boys gathering for a game of stickball.

"Wait for me fellas!" The boys jeered, but Donny seemed satisfied that they would wait at least a little while.

Patty opened the kitchen door and instructed Lily and Donny to place the baskets on the table. Delicious aromas of stews and pies Patty filled with meats bathed the kitchen. Lily's stomach rolled with hunger.

"Who's this wee lassie?" asked Patty, reaching for Gigi's long braids.

"This is my little sister, Gigi. I have to mind her today, so she is tagging along," said Lily. Gigi shyly looked up at Patty's freckled face smile.

"Lily, would ya' collect 'da money 'n bring back to Mr. Goldberg?" asked Donny, "I wanna get to 'da game."

Lily sighed in agreement. She would never get home and shake Gigi loose today. And it's Sunday. She had hoped to play with Nelly today.

"I'll fetch Miss Wald," said Patty.

"Come on Gigi, help me count the bread." Lily took one

round loaf of bread out of the basket. Her bread song stirred. She took in a delicious breath and sang out:

One crusty bread, all alone, feeling blue
Another comes along, now there are two
Two crusty breads tasty as can be
Another comes along, now there's three.
Three crusty breads, are there any more?

Lily liked the way her voice sounded in the kitchen, lined with bricks and a flagstone floor. Her notes filled the room.

"More! More!" chimed Gigi, holding up the fourth loaf of bread.

"Another comes along, now there are four!" Lily's song thundered. She added hand flourish, the way Mrs. Goldberg showed her. Gigi laughed.

Miss Wald walked through the door. "My goodness, is that voice coming from you?"

Lily gulped and placed the fourth loaf of bread gently on the table. "Sorry, ma'am. I didn't realize I was so loud."

"Nonsense," said Miss Wald, "Powerful. You have a powerful voice. Never apologize for a powerful voice."

"Each time I see this young lass, she carries a joyful song in her heart, she does," said Patty, walking in behind Miss Wald.

"How old are you, child? Eleven? Twelve?" asked Miss Wald.

"Nine," replied Lily, "I'll be ten at the end of the summer."

"So tall for your age," said Miss Wald.

"My papa is tall. Betta and me take after Papa. And I do exercises with Mrs. Goldberg to help my bones and muscles grow straight and tall." Lily did not want to say the exercises were for ballerinas. Mrs. Goldberg's ballerina past was a secret.

"Yes, I heard about that," said Miss Wald. "I also understand your baby sister is growing and sleeping better now that she is supplemented. Your sister, Betta, is feeling stronger."

"Yes ma'am," said Lily.

"And how is your mother faring? Miss Forsythe reports she continues to feel poorly and despondent."

Lily wasn't sure what despondent meant but was sure Mama would not want anyone to know that she was still weak.

"She's better," fibbed Lily.

"Of course," said Miss Wald. Lily patted her smock down and tucked a stray hair behind her ear.

Miss Wald turned to Patty. "Miss O'Shea, please ask Miss Lowen to meet me in the yard?" Patty disappeared, and Miss Wald turned to Lily and Gigi. "Follow me, please."

Lily collected the empty baskets and took Gigi's hand.

"Be quiet," whispered Lily, although Gigi was usually quiet. It was more of a reminder to herself.

CHAPTER 12
THE PLAYGROUND

MISS WALD LED the girls into the house and up a short flight of stairs. Lily noticed the bright hallway and stairwell. Her tenement hallways and staircases were dark with ghostly shadows. Miss Wald stopped at a door that led to an enclosed courtyard.

"Mind the steps," she said.

A wall covered with purple wisteria climbing on a trellis enclosed the yard. Yellow day lilies and pretty red and orange flowers grew along the edges. Green vines and pink flowers hung from window boxes. In a shaded corner, there was a sand pile, a swing set with three scuppers, and gymnastic equipment. A small group of girls chanted while sharing a long jumping rope. Boys played catch and tag.

There was a playground at Seward Park, just a few blocks away from 125 Mott Street. It had swings and slides and plenty of space to play tag. Lily and Gigi were not allowed to go to the park. Papa said children disappeared in the parks.

"Why Papa?" asked Lily. "Why would someone snatch me or Nelly or Gigi?"

Papa did not answer. He looked hard at Lily and made her promise that she would not play in the park without Margaret or Mama with her. The stern look convinced Lily to not ask again. The front stoop was a good enough place for the girls to play. Margaret nor Mama never had time to go to the park.

"Scuppers!" shouted Gigi, "Can I swing?"

"Go right ahead," said Miss Wald, "This is a safe place for children to play."

"We have to go home," said Lily.

"Bring your sister to the swings and wait for me," said Miss Wald. "I'll bring you the bakery money. I'd like for you to meet someone."

Gigi did not wait for Lily to agree. She ran down the steps and climbed on an empty swing scupper between two little boys. Lily sighed and followed Gigi.

"It will be for just a few minutes," reasoned Lily to herself, "Then we'll drop off the money and go home. Mama should not worry. Papa should not be mad since this is the Settlement's yard, not a city playground."

Gigi kicked her legs back and forth.

"Put your legs out straight," instructed Lily. "I'll push you." Gigi squealed with joy, reaching her legs in the air. She leaned back. Her long braids followed close behind.

"Fold your legs back," called Lily. Gigi swung back. Lily gave her another push and off she flew, reaching her legs to the sky in a trail of laughter. The little boy on the right side kicked his feet furiously, attempting to catch up with Gigi. Lily gave him a gentle push. Up he soared in a trail of joy. The boy on the left scupper sat quietly, watching Gigi and the other boy. His hair was the color of carrots, and brown freckles covered his face.

"Would you like a push?" asked Lily.

The carrot-hair boy nodded his head and gripped the side ropes tightly.

"Reach with your legs," said Lily.

The carrot-hair boy kicked out his right leg. His left leg hung down uselessly. Lily spied a crutch leaning against the swing set. She smiled at the boy and gave him a big push. Within minutes, all three children were whooping and cheering as they swung back and forth. Lily had to sing.

Swinging Swinging
Watch me go Swinging Swinging
See me go Swinging Swinging
Here I swing up, then back again

Lily knew her voice was loud—powerful as she pushed the little kids. She gave an extra boost to the carrot-hair boy. Another voice joined her song. She stopped singing and noticed that all the children in the yard were watching her. A delicate young woman with soft brown hair tied into a tight bun at the nape of her neck picked up Lily's tune. She wore a plain beige dress that covered her neck and arms and fell to her ankles. It was difficult to see her eyes since they were deeply set back. She had a tiny upturned nose and thin lips that blended into the same hue of her pale complexion. Her voice harmonized with Lily in a high register. It was thin, yet clear.

The woman applauded Lily, which encouraged the other children to clap, except for the three still swinging. Lily did not know if she should curtsy, like the ballerina curtsies Mrs. Goldberg taught her, or remain standing, savoring the little thrill. She never got an applause from a group before. Clapping for the school assemblies was discouraged. "We do not sing patriotic songs to cultivate conceit," explained Mr. Ross, the school principal.

"Swinging! Swinging!" shouted Gigi. Lily shook her head. Gigi did not have a singing voice.

"You are so right, Miss Wald," said the plain woman, "This girl has a powerful voice beyond her years."

Miss Wald nodded. "Miss Martha Lowen, meet Lily Taglia, nine years old, almost ten."

"Fantastic!" said Miss Lowen, holding out her right hand. Lily now knew how to shake a hand.

"Nice to meet you, Lily," said Miss Lowen. "Would you like to join the Children's Choir here at the Henry Street Settlement? It is a lovely group of youngsters making beautiful music. We sing modern and classic songs together. Practice is on Wednesday afternoons, promptly at four o'clock."

"I don't know," stammered Lily.

"You can bring your little sister. She can play in the yard with the children while you sing. There is always someone watching. It is perfectly safe," continued Miss Lowen.

"There is no cost to your family," said Miss Wald. "We, at Henry Street Settlement, believe it is important to encourage music, art and play. Nurturing the soul is key to a successful life. We host dances and concerts for the neighborhood. The Children's Choir is very popular."

As much as Lily wanted to sing, her mind flooded with obstacles. There was laundry to fold and errands to run. She had to carry howling Violet. Gigi always hung on her skirt and Margaret always found something for her to do. She had to do everything! But to sing new songs was an exciting invitation.

CHAPTER 13
RUDE EDITH

A SHRILLY "YOOHOO!" disconnected Lily's racing thought. The call came from the top of the steps. A tall girl with yellow hair that fell in soft curls, waved her arm toward Miss Wald. She wore a blue dress and black shoes that shone in the spring sunlight. Her curls bounced on her shoulders as she clattered down the stairs. The girl's green eyes squinted in the sunlight and her full lips matched the rosy glow in her cheeks.

"There you are, Cousin Lillian," said the girl breathlessly.

Miss Wald turned to the girl. "Edith, you are interrupting."

Edith wriggled her slender hand into a white glove. "What am I interrupting? It's just a bunch of kids."

"Miss Lowen and I are speaking to this young lady. You interrupted and need to apologize."

The girl smoothed the glove on her arm and glanced to the side of Miss Wald. "Yes, Cousin Lillian. I did not see Miss Lowen. I beg your pardon."

The apology did not sound sincere. The children resumed their play. Lily helped Gigi off the scupper seat.

"Cousin Lillian, you said I may go for a walk in the park this afternoon. It is such a lovely afternoon," said Edith. She pulled on the matching white glove. "I finished sorting the handbills."

"Did you finish arranging the chairs in the parlor?"

"Yes, Cousin Lillian. Honestly, don't the servants do that sort of thing?"

Miss Wald stepped closer to the rude girl. "My dear Edith, this is not a playhouse for your entertainment. You are here at your mother's, my dear cousin, behest. She wants you to cultivate a sense of compassion and appreciation, just as she and I were raised. Everyone here pitches in to better the lives of the community, and, in turn, the city, the state, and our great country."

"Yes, Cousin Lillian," said Edith.

Miss Wald sighed and turned to Lily.

"Lily Taglia, meet my cousin, Edith Reicher," said Miss Wald.

"Nice to meet you," said Lily. She held out her right hand to Edith. Edith reluctantly tapped Lily's fingertips with her gloved hand.

"Hello," mumbled the girl.

"We were awed at Lily's singing voice," said Miss Lowen, "She would be a wonderful addition to our choir."

Edith nodded, then brought her attention back to her gloves.

"I have to ask my mama," said Lily.

"Of course, dear," said Miss Wald.

Miss Wald walked Lily and Gigi to the gate that opened onto the street. She gave Lily an envelope for the bread payment and pressed two nickels into her palm.

"For you and Donny's delivery service," she whispered.

"Thank you, Miss Wald. And thank you for inviting me to the choir, but there is a lot to do with the new baby and Mama, being so, er, Mama not being herself, yet."

"I understand," said Miss Wald, "I look forward to seeing you on Wednesday afternoon."

CHAPTER 14

THICKHEADED THEA AND STICKBALL

GIGI SKIPPED ALONGSIDE LILY. Lily held fast to Gigi with one hand and the envelope and nickels in her pinafore pocket with the other. She would have liked to buy a peppermint stick for Mama, her sisters, and herself, but knew she should add the nickel to the coffee can. They retraced their route through the alley and into Seward Park.

Lily spotted the stickball game. Donny stood against a lamppost, clapping and shouting at the players.

"Are you playing?" asked Lily. Gigi lightly panted, swinging Lily's arm.

"Nah, 'dah boys got someone else to cover for me," said Donny.

"Who?"

Donny pointed toward a kid holding a stick that might have belonged to a broom or mop. The batter was short and skinny and faced the thrower sideways in a crouched position. Lily took another look. The batter was wearing a skirt with an apron on top! Long black tendrils spilled out of a brown cap that was obviously too big for her head. She wore the visor backward, so her dark eyes and long nose faced the thrower.

"That's Thea Christopoulos," said Lily.

"Yeah, Thickheaded Thea," said Donny, kicking a can into the street gutter. "Yanni's sista'."

Thea was in Margaret's class. She was short, but her lean body was fast and strong. She could outrun all the girls and most of the boys in the eighth-year class. Margaret said she was always moving, even while sitting. Her leg constantly bounced up and down, ready to pounce into action.

"And her penmanship is terrible," said Margaret, "The teacher makes her redo writing assignments, which makes her steaming mad."

Thea worked in her family's general store. She easily lugged sacks of goods and climbed stacks of shelves. The store carried everything and anything. If an item was not there, Mrs. Christopoulos happily ordered it and had it in the store within a week.

Thea's sleeves were rolled past her elbows. She pulled the back of her skirt to the front and tucked it into the waistband to create a pantaloon. Lily saw she could probably run faster without worrying about her skirt.

"Come on! Ya' call that a pitch," hollered Thea to the thrower. Her deep voice bellowed off the building walls.

Donny kicked another can off the curb. "They let her play 'cause she's Yanni's sista'—the best stickball playa' of all time."

"Is Yanni here?" asked Lily, stretching to look over the gaggle of boys. "Did he come back?" Lily remembered Yanni as tall and skinny, with a head full of unruly black curls. He organized kids to play in alleys. When he wasn't playing stickball, he bounced and caught a ball off the General Store wall. He taught Thea how to hit a ball with a broomstick. Playing baseball was all he thought and talked about.

Yanni's father had enough of his ball-playing when Yanni started spending time with leagues in the parks. He would leave his chores and hop a ferry to Staten Island and sometimes New Jersey to play.

Yanni had not been home since last summer. There were rumors that his father, a gruff man with a gravelly voice, burned Yanni's mitt and sent him to live with relatives in Greece or, perhaps, upstate. Some boys claimed Yanni jumped a train and became a cowboy riding horses and lassoing steers. Now that he was almost eighteen years old, he could be anywhere. Thea kept her family business to herself and did not offer any clues. She had enough to do helping her mother and avoiding her father's temper. But, like her brother, she loved to play ball.

A crack echoed from the alley.

"Look at 'dat!" whined Donny. "A home run." Thea sped to a can cover, tagged a burlap bag, stepped on a flour sack, then raced to a flattened cardboard box where she started. She careened into Big John before he caught the ball.

"She batted in two fellas and herself," said Donny. "I ain't gonna get a chance to play today. 'Dere should be a rule against girls playing ball."

"Why?" asked Lily. "It looks like Thea can play just as good as the boys, maybe better."

Donny shrugged. "Don't get me started about ladies' doing men's work. Girls shouldn't play a man's game when 'dey got plenty to do otherwise."

"So girls shouldn't do anything fun?" asked Lily.

"No, uh, uh, ain't cookin' and sewin' fun?" Donny pretended to watch the stickball game.

"Better not let Margaret hear you talk like that. She might punch you in the nose," said Lily.

Donny rubbed his nose and grinned. "Yeah, I'm careful around Margaret."

"Are you a good stickball player, Donny?"

Donny kicked another can into the gutter. "Not like 'dat gal on account of seeing cock-eyed with this crooked face."

Months ago, Donny told Lily of the time when a gang of bullies beat him. Big John came to his rescue. He chased the bad boys away and took Donny to the sisters at the convent. It took a while, but they patched him up as best they could. The right side of Donny's face drooped, and his eyelid covered half of the right eye. Since Donny and Big John became friends with Lily and Margaret, Lily barely noticed Donny's disfigurement.

"Ya know, baseball is 'da greatest," said Donny. "One of 'dese days, I'm gonna see a real game, maybe at 'da Polo Grounds. 'Dem Giants fixed up 'da field real nice. Maybe get me a job at 'da field, meet 'da boys, get some tips. Maybe one of 'dem know a trick or two so I could keep me eye on 'da ball."

Lily smiled. "It's a nice dream."

Donny shrugged again. "Come on. I'll walk ya' back to 'da bakery."

"I have to get Gigi home. Mama will be worried," said Lily, "Can you take the delivery money? Oh, here is your tip from Miss Wald."

"Sure," said Donny. He turned to the stickball game.

"Hold your elbow up higher and keep your eye on the ball," shouted Thea. "I ain't babysittin' your swelled head!"

"Look at 'dat," said Donny, "She can pitch, too."

Gigi swung her arm, holding onto Lily's hand. "Swing. Swing. Swing up. Swing back."

Lily shook her head. "You have the words all mixed up."

"Let's play outside, Lily. I don't wanna go upstairs," said Gigi, standing at the bottom of their stoop steps.

"We have to go home. Mama will be mad," said Lily.

"No," said Gigi, "Mama don't get mad no more. Mama don't get happy no more. Baby Violet makes her sad."

"That's not true, Gigi," said Lily, "Mama is tired. Miss Forsythe said so."

Gigi shook her head. "Violet makes Mama sad. She's a bad baby. Let's give that baby away."

"Don't say such a thing! Violet is our sister, Mama and Papa's baby. You'll see. Soon she'll be smiling and laughing and goo-gooing at you."

Gigi stuck her thumb into her mouth and knitted her dark eyebrows into a frown. "Bad baby," she mumbled, "Give her away."

CHAPTER 15
A DRESS FROM CONNIE

Voices burst out of the Taglia door. Lily and Gigi entered a crowd of bodies and noise crammed into the front room. Mama sat in Papa's big chair by the window with Papa standing over her. Nelly and her grandmother, Nonna, sat on the couch with Betta holding the baby between them. Zia Giaconda, Connie's mother, sat in a chair in the middle of the room. Her three young toddlers clamored over each other at her feet. Margaret stood over Connie's mother, holding a bolt of snow-white material close to her chest.

Gigi shook Lily's hand loose and raced for Mama's lap. Mama looked down at Gigi, tears streaming down her tired face. Lily was getting used to seeing Mama quietly weep since Violet was born, but these were different tears.

"What's going on?" asked Lily.

"It is wonderful," exclaimed Betta, "Zia Giaconda gave Margaret material to sew a Moving Up dress."

Margaret turned to show Lily the bright material. Her eyes were rimmed red with tears.

"Zia Giaconda says that Margaret needs a new dress for moving up from 8th grade to high school," continued Betta, "especially since she is going to receive the High Honor

Award. She is going to sit front and center on the stage, so she will need to look her best."

The Moving Up ceremony required 8th-year students to wear clean clothing—no tatters. Mama agreed Margaret needed a new dress and offered to sew it for her once the new baby came. But since Violet's birth, Mama could not start. Margaret had to sew it herself.

Margaret hoped for a bright dress, but they could only afford dull muslin material. Money was tight without Mama keeping up with the sewing homework. Her baskets of cuffs and collars overflowed. Papa brought home enough to pay the rent and put food, as meager as it was, on the table. The expenses of a new baby left little for extras, like fabric for a dress. Margaret and Betta contributed their pennies, but the home budget was still tight.

Margaret settled on the dull muslin. She finished the high neck bodice with pleated sleeves at the shoulders that gently tapered to an elegant cuff at the wrist. It hung against the wardrobe door in the front room. A skirt, long enough to reach her ankles, lay folded in a basket waiting to be attached. If she had enough time, Margaret planned to embroider roses and vines around the cuffs and neckline. But with school, the bakery, the new baby, and Mama, not herself, there was little time.

"My Carlo, Connie's papa, bartered for this fabric," said Zia Giaconda, "He fixed the basement for the Christopoulos' store. My Carlo could fix and build most anything. Remember Stefano?"

Papa nodded at the memory of his friend.

"He wanted our Freddo to be an Americana boy and Connie an Americana girl. We couldn't make a life at home, Sicilia. No hope to work toward. So we take what little we had, and bring our children and memories to America. That's why we come."

"There is a dream for everyone willing to work in America. My daughters can have a good life," said Papa.

"That dream is dead for my daughter," said Zia Giaconda, "My Carlo got killed by a factory machine and Connie burned in the Triangle Shirtwaist fire. The new husband kicked my Freddo out. Old enough to fend for himself, he says."

Everyone nodded at the sad truths.

"It's beautiful," sniffed Margaret. "I will make a dress Connie would be proud to wear."

"Connie didn't like school," said Zia Giaconda, "Not like you, Margaret. Her papa would have been proud to see her finish the eighth grade, perhaps go to high school, like the Americana girls. But this new husband made it difficult. She had to—Stop! Stop you brute boys!" Zia Giaconda swatted at her little boys who were tumbling onto each other, screeching and crying.

Nonna stood up and stroked the bolt. "Such fine quality. It is a generous gift."

Nonna loomed large over Margaret and Zia Giaconda in the middle of the room. She had a happy, full face despite the weary bags under her eyes and sweat pooling from her temples and dark upper lip. Lily never saw Nonna's hair tamed into a smooth bun, even for Mass. Damp strings of brown and grey surrounded the woman's head and framed her wide face. Her blouse had sweat stains around the neck and arms and sometimes her back from pressing garments for the home sweatshop.

Unlike the Taglia's home and most of the apartments in the tenement, Nelly and Nonna were the only ones living in their three-room apartment. Nelly's papa died from contracting consumption from boarders who lived in the little apartment with them. Later that year, Nelly's mama passed away giving birth to a stillborn baby boy, but Nelly believed she died of a broken heart. Nonna decided she will never let strangers live in her home ever again. Instead, she would work like a horse to keep Nelly and her safe.

Nonna worked for the Jewish family sweatshop in the tenement. The family worked ten hours a day, six days a week, sewing piece work on foot pedal machines. Nonna was the presser, a job her husband had before he died in his sleep four years before. She had enough strength and skill to lift the hot cast-iron weights and iron even pleats and smocking without burning delicate fabric. Although tragedy followed her and she was always ironing, Nonna had a kind voice and a loud laugh. She insisted the children call her Nonna.

"I will have to work fast," said Margaret. "Moving Up Day is three weeks away."

Nonna rubbed the fabric between her thumb and index finger. "It is a fine thread." She took the fabric from Margaret and showed it to Mama. "See Cesca? I will ask the tailor if Margaret could use the machine on Friday night and Saturday. It is their Sabbath. They can't work a machine on their Sabbath. It will make the job quick."

"Se," said Mama softly without touching the material.

Papa smiled and put his hand on Mama's shoulder.

"Perhaps you can crochet a delicate pattern along the neckline," suggested Nonna.

"Se," repeated Mama.

"I bought a pink ribbon today," said Margaret pulling it from her apron pocket, "I thought I'd sew it at the waist."

Mama nodded. A tear dropped on top of Gigi's head.

"Thank you, Giaconda," said Papa, "Connie is smiling from heaven."

Zia Giaconda dragged one of her boys toward Mama and looked at her friend. Lily noticed they shared the same sad eyes.

"Get well, my dear friend," whispered Zia Giaconda. "Your daughters carry the hope and dreams of this new life. And you have this good man willing to work with you. Take good care of them." She stroked Gigi's head. "Especially my little namesake here."

Mama sniffed and nodded.

Zia Giaconda shook her squirming child. "Amunninni ! Let's go," Zia Giaconda said to the squabbling trio, "I have to go home to make supper for your brute of a father."

Zia Giaconda and the children shouted and scuffled as they scrambled down the stairs. Lily closed the door. Home was instantly quiet.

CHAPTER 16
BASEBALL CARDS IN CIGARETTE BOXES

"What took you so long, Songbird?" asked Papa.

Lily was about to explain that she had to wait for Miss Wald to pay the bakery bill, but Gigi piped up. "We played on the swings!"

"You played in the park?" asked Margaret.

"No, uh, Gigi, uh no," sputtered Lily.

"It is dangerous for little girls to go to the park by themselves," said Papa, "You are not allowed to play there."

Mama hugged Gigi to her chest. "Dark hands. Must stay close to home."

"But Mama, Henry Street Settlement has a closed-in yard with swings and a place to play," explained Lily, "I was with Gigi. Nothing happened."

"Mama, you're squishing me," whined Gigi.

Mama looked at Lily with her sad eyes. Gigi wiggled in her clutch. "Evil in the parks," whispered Mama.

Lily happily braced herself for a volley of the real Mama's wrath. Would her temper rise and voice holler? Perhaps Mama was coming back to her old self. Instead. Mama deflated with a sigh and released Gigi. She fell back into Papa's chair.

Papa sighed, too. He seemed just as disappointed as Lily. "Don't bring Gigi to any park or yard."

"But Papa," whined Gigi.

"No!" barked Papa, pointing his finger at Gigi.

Tony walked into the kitchen from the hall. He held up a card to Papa. "Zio, look what I found in Joe's cigarette box."

Papa examined the picture on the card.

"They put these baseball cards in cigarette boxes," explained Tony.

"Why?" asked Papa.

Tony shrugged. "You trade them with other kids or collect them. But look at the card, Zio, See?"

Papa looked again at the card. "It is Curly Crisp. He's the new Yankee on the New York Highlanders."

"Look again. Don't he look familiar?"

Lily and Margaret looked over Papa's shoulder.

"Hey, it's Yanni Christopoulos!" said Margaret.

The photograph showed a young man smiling and holding a baseball bat and wearing a cap with NY on the front. Dark, curly hair hung above his thick eyebrows.

"Yanni is a Yankee Highlander. He is Curly Crisp!" said Tony.

"That is so keen!" exclaimed Lily, "His papa will be proud of him now."

Nonna lumbered into the kitchen and took the card from Papa. "He gave up his name to play a game? He turned his back on who he is?" asked Nonna.

"Yanni Christopoulos is a hard name to say even for a Greek," said Papa, "Americanas like to make names simple. Lily's name is Laboria, but here everyone calls her Lily. Nelly is Angelina. A simple name makes it easy to go to school, get a job."

Nonna shook her large head. "A game is a poor excuse to turn your back on a family name."

Nonna handed the card back to Tony. Mama shuffled into the kitchen.

"Evil," whispered Mama, "Evil is all around this horrible place."

"Stop it, Cesca!" Papa's voice boomed. Violet whimpered in Betta's arms.

Mama returned to the front room and sat in Papa's chair.

"I just wanted to show Zio baseball cards in cigarette boxes," said Tony inching to the door, "So you can know the players. I gotta go."

"Antonino, come downstairs with me," said Nonna. "I got escarole and beans on the stove. Too much for Nelly and me."

Lily closed the door when she heard Nonna, Nelly, and Tony stepped down the stairwell to the third floor. Violet shrilled. Betta poured evaporated milk into a bottle. Gigi flopped on the cot next to the stove, stuck her thumb in her mouth, and mumbled, "Bad baby."

CHAPTER 17
SNEAKY SECRETS

Wednesday, May 24, 1911

A WEEK HAD GONE by since Miss Wald and Miss Lowen asked Lily to sing in the choir. Lily was no closer to asking Mama for permission.

Miss Triptree chose Joshua to solve 62 ⟌ 3,479 in front of the entire class on the blackboard.

"Use your right hand," warned Miss Triptree.

The long division problem stared at Lily from her slate. The numbers would not stay in place and she mixed the multiplication and subtraction steps. It was hard to concentrate. Getting to the Henry Street Settlement choir practice was a bigger problem.

The night before, Lily tried to explain to Mama that the Henry Street Settlement playground was closed off to the streets and children could play safely. Mama mumbled about evil in the neighborhood. Violet wailed. Gigi sobbed. Margaret stomped about and Betta held her head. Papa could not find peace in his home, so he tucked a cigar in his pocket, put on his cap, and headed for the roof.

Lily confided in Nelly. "It's not fair. My sisters get what they want all the time. Margaret gets attention for how smart and clever she is, Betta has her books, and Gigi can play all the time. Everyone gets to be special, except me! I really want to sing in the choir, but I'm afraid Mama and Papa will say no."

"Perhaps after school you can go on an errand for Mrs. Goldberg," said Nelly. "You can say it was a long walk, or that there was a long line."

"I'd have to take Gigi like I always do after school. She'll slow me down."

"Perhaps if I came with you, we can move Gigi along faster," said Nelly, twisting her pinafore, "Then perhaps I can sing in the choir, too."

"Oh Nelly, that would be grand!" said Lily. "I am sure Miss Lowen would love for you to sing in the choir, too." She suddenly felt badly that she did not think of her friend sooner. "But you can't ask Nonna until I ask Mama and Papa."

Lily tried to get advice from Margaret.

"You know that sneaky secrets have a way of getting out," said Margaret, "And how do you suppose Gigi won't blabber?"

"Gigi won't wreck her chances playing on the playground," said Lily.

Margaret set her mouth in a tight line and shook her head.

Lily discussed the problem with Mrs. Goldberg. Although a grown-up, Mrs. Goldberg would understand how important it was for Lily to sing in a choir.

"Yes, yes. Very good sing in choir. But must not worry Mama, my friend. Must not disobey Papa."

~

Lily sighed at the long division problem. No one had the answer she wanted.

Joshua solved the long division problem in less than a minute. He lined up the place values, multiplied, subtracted, borrowed, and wrote the correct answer with his right hand. He announced the answer without a stammer and gave a little bow. Lily could see how much his heart swelled with pride. She wanted to clap but thought better of it. Miss Triptree would be cross and ruin Joshua's triumph.

A good plan never emerged while the class recited the seven and eight multiplication facts. Miss Triptree wrote $76\overline{)2052}$ on the blackboard. Lily shrank her head toward her desk, trying to disappear from the yardstick pointing toward her. It worked. Miss Triptree's stick missed Lily but pointed at Nelly. Nelly's face grew pale.

"Let's see what you know, girl," sneered Miss Triptree.

Poor Nelly, who did not know all the multiplication facts and could not possibly figure such a big problem with her fingers, stood facing the blackboard, unable to start. Miss Triptree sauntered down Lily's row, peering at the students' work on their slates.

Lily wished she could swoop Nelly out of the room. They could run from Miss Triptree's class, out of the school, and hide—perhaps in the Goldberg's bakery.

Mrs. Goldberg would probably enjoy the excitement. She may even find a secret corner to tuck away in. But Mr. Goldberg would arch his right or left eyebrow, tsk his tongue, then list all the reasons why they could not hide from Miss Triptree and long division. Besides, Margaret would find them and mercilessly scold and drag them back to school to apologize. They would endure ruler smacks to their knuckles and spend midday and after school completing multiplication and long division drills on the blackboard.

Lily looked up at Miss Triptree staring at her slate. The large woman pushed up her wire-rimmed glasses and shook her head. Lily had not begun to solve the problem.

"It's impossible to teach these backward immigrants," mumbled the teacher. She lumbered to the front of the classroom.

"Sit down, Nelly. You're wasting our time. It's obvious you have no mind for this. You are destined to remain ignorant and a burden to society."

Nelly placed the chalk on the blackboard ledge and swallowed a sob. She cast her eyes down as she made a way back to her seat.

The noon-day bell rescued the class. Lily scrambled out of her seat but Nelly sat still, her eyes gazed down, hiding a pool of tears. Lily gently shook her friend.

"Come to the bakery with me, Nelly. Mr. Goldberg won't mind you watching me knead and shape Daily Bread."

Nelly and Lily walked arm-in-arm down Baxter Street. They strolled just a few steps behind Mita and Margaret. Lily could see that Mita was jabbering.

"She's a worse magpie than Connie ever was," complained Margaret one night.

Nelly and Lily usually talked incessantly when they were together. If they weren't talking, they sang. Nelly's voice was silvery and sweet as opposed to Lily's robust and rich sound that traveled through rooms and doors and into the street. Margaret said Lily sang loud and bawdy. Papa said he liked how Lily's hearty voice mixed with his when they sang opera arias and Sicilian folk songs together. Miss Wald and Miss Lowen called Lily's voice powerful. Lily liked the word powerful.

This afternoon, Nelly was silent. She barely noticed friends along the way. Lily pulled her out of the path of an enormous pile of horse droppings in the gutter. Nelly usually did that for Lily.

"Don't believe that mean old Miss Triptree," said Lily. "We are going to grow up smart, get out of this stinking neighborhood and make our own American dreams. "

"We're not too smart with figures like Joshua and Margaret," said Nelly.

Lily shrugged. "That's okay. We're smart in other ways."

"Like what?"

"Like making up songs, singing in tune. Margaret's voice is so flat. Papa shakes his head when Margaret tries to sing with us."

Nelly smiled. "She is an awful singer."

"Betta reads everything and wants to write poetry, but she can't run," continued Lily.

"That's true," said Nelly, "I can embroider and crochet better than you."

"Anyone, even Gigi, can embroider and crochet better than me," giggled Lily. "Everyone has an artist's heart in something. You just have to find what makes your heart proud and happy. Then practice it and love it to make it your own. That's what Mrs. Goldberg says. I love to sing so I need to practice, somehow."

The friends skipped down the bakery basement steps.

Mrs. Goldberg snatched Lily off the last step of the basement.

"Come Lily," she whispered, "Have plan."

CHAPTER 18

MRS. GOLDBERG'S PLAN

Mrs. Goldberg came up with a plan that was almost honest rather than entirely sneaky. After school on Wednesdays, Lily would pick up her Daily Bread, just like every afternoon. She would also have to deliver a basket with two loaves of bread and a half dozen Knot Surprises to the Henry Street Settlement.

"Miss Wald sweet tooth beg for Knot Surprise," said Mrs. Goldberg. "Most customer like Mama, my friend, strawberry jam on top, but all gone. Cinnamon and sugar good enough. Yes?"

Mama usually jarred strawberries by the dozen in June. But since she continued to feel weak and tired, it was not certain if there would be any strawberry jam to sell to the Goldbergs.

Lily and Nelly would bring the Daily Bread to Mama. They could not play with Gigi on the stoop because they had to deliver the basket of bread to Miss Wald. The girls would run to the Henry Street Settlement, deliver the breadbasket to Patty, and arrive in time to sing in the choir.

Margaret listened to this plan with her lips in a tight line. She did not like the secret.

"Papa won't like this and Mama will be spitting mad if she found out. And what about Gigi? She will make everyone crazy if she can't tag along."

Lily shook her head at Margaret. She wanted to tell her it would be grand to see Mama spitting mad rather than quiet and sad. Instead, she said that Betta can take Gigi outside and that she would play with Gigi when she got home. Promise. Margaret shook her head.

"You are taking advantage of Mama's melancholy," said Margaret.

"Please, Margaret, please don't tell. I kept your secret. I swore to God that I would not tell Mama you saved bread money to prove you could earn while going to school. Remember how mad Mama got when you had the money to pay the doctor. Papa needed an operation after that awful fight on the docks. You had the money to pay the doctor who would not talk to the police."

Lily would never forget that horrible night when Papa's partner, Sam, hid Papa for a day. There was trouble on the pier that had to do with fair wages for longshoremen, including the Italians who barely spoke English and the Negros. Traps and knife fights broke out. Papa or Sam may have killed a worker who attacked them. When it was safe, Sam, a huge colored man, draped Papa across his broad shoulders, carried him home from alley to alley, and lay the beaten body on the kitchen table. Blood poured from deep wounds. Margaret fetched the quack doctor, who vowed silence for a price. The doctor saved Papa, but Mama called Margaret a thief for paying the doctor with secret money.

Everyone thought Margaret ran away to find Connie and join her working in a factory. Instead, the Goldbergs madeher stay in their apartment to cool off. It was fortunate because the next day the devastating fire at the Triangle Shirtwaist Factory burned swiftly and trapped young women in flames and smoke. Connie was one of the many girls who jumped to her death from the ninth floor, engulfed in fire. Mama was so relieved to see Margaret. She forgave Margaret for saving the money.

~

"If anything happens just because you want to sing, Mama may never forgive you. Papa will never trust you again," said Margaret.

"I'm going to deliver bread, sing a few songs, then go home," said Lily. "I will keep Gigi from making everyone crazy when I get home. I promise. Just please, please don't tell."

Margaret looked over at Mrs. Goldberg packing the basket. The woman hummed an aimless tune and rocked on her toes. She lay a linen towel over the bread, then turned to pass the basket to Lily. Her cheeks glittered with sugar.

"Alright," sighed Margaret, "I promise."

"Swear to God?" asked Lily, hefting the basket.

Margaret's deep brown eyes glared at Lily. She looked like Mama used to. "I swear to God," she mumbled, "You make me crazy!"

CHAPTER 19
A CHANGE OF PLANS

LILY CARRIED the basket of bread and Knot Surprises and Nelly toted the Daily Bread in her hands. They found Betta, Gigi, and Tony sitting on the front stoop. The sun shone on Betta's hair, sparkling pretty reflections of gold and red. Each day she was feeling stronger and hadn't had a headache in almost a week. Gigi ran up to Lily, almost knocking over Signore Costa carrying a bag of potatoes on the crowded sidewalk.

"Hey, watch out!" shouted the old man.

"Scusa," squeaked Lily, "She's just a little kid."

"Should keep that little kid on a leash!" said Signore Costa. "The Black Hand grabs one so small."

Lily and Nelly watched Signore Costa waddle across the street, blending into the congestion of people, carts, horses, and motor cars.

"What is a Black Hand?" asked Nelly.

"Maybe it's a fairy tale, like a boogeyman, to scare kids into behaving," said Lily.

"Oh no, it's real," said Betta, "They are terrible people, who take small children and make their families pay for their return."

Tony kicked a pebble off the stoop. "They snatch little kids whose parents work steady, so they know who can pay."

"They could be our neighbors. It is too scary to imagine. It is scarier than any fairytales I read," said Betta,

Gigi pulled on Lily's skirt. "Come on, Lily. Let's play."

Lily thought no hand was going to want to take her sticky, whiny little sister who is wet with spit. "I can't," said Lily, "I have to deliver this basket to Henry Street-"

"I go! I go, too! We can swing!" exclaimed Gigi, hanging onto Lily's arm.

"No, I can't take you," said Lily, shaking Gigi off of her arm, "Nelly and I have to hurry."

"I want to go!" shouted Gigi. She stamped her little feet.

"You can't. I have a job!"

"No, No, No!" screamed Gigi, "I will tell Mama. I will tell Papa you are singing at the big house."

So Gigi was paying attention when Miss Wald and Miss Lowen offered Lily to join the choir. Lily looked up to the fourth-floor window. Mama was not staring out hearing Gigi's tantrum, yet. It was hopeless. Lily did not have time to argue. She had to tell Betta and Tony about the choir and how Mrs. Goldberg gave her an errand to deliver bread and Knot Surprises so she could sing in the choir.

"Please don't tell Mama."

Gigi stomped her foot. "I go. I swing. You sing."

"I can't sing if you are in the playground," said Lily.

Tony jumped off the last two steps of the stoop. "I'll go with you. I'll keep an eye on Gigi while you sing."

"You'd do that?" asked Lily.

"Sure. I got nothing else to do," said Tony, taking Gigi's hand.

Gigi happily jumped up and down. "Hurray! Hurray!"

"You can't tell Mama and Papa you were swinging on scuppers," said Lily.

Gigi stuck her thumb in her mouth and nodded her head.

"You have to promise," said Nelly.

Gigi nodded again.

"You have to say it," said Lily.

"I pomisth," said Gigi through her thumb-filled mouth.

"You have to swear to God," said Lily, "If you break the promise, God will punish you."

Gigi looked up at her sister with big brown eyes and popped out her thumb. "What will God do to me if I tell?"

Lily let out an exasperated sigh. Why were little sisters so difficult?

Tony crouched down to Gigi's eye level. "I'm not sure, but no one has lived to tell what God did to them after they broke a swear to God promise." Gigi's eyes widened. She put her thumb back in her mouth and sucked harder.

"Say it, Gigi," demanded Lily. "Take that disgusting thumb out of your mouth so we can all hear you, including God."

Gigi slowly took her thumb out of her mouth and put both hands behind her back.

"I promise. I swear to God I won't tell."

CHAPTER 20
SINGING AND SWINGING

PLANS CHANGED. Betta took the loaf of Daily Bread upstairs. She would report to Mama and Nonna that Lily, Nelly, Tony, were delivering for the Goldbergs and were taking Gigi along.

Patty opened the kitchen door for the children. "Oh such angelic sight!" exclaimed Patty.

Gigi pulled Tony through the kitchen. "This way!"

Patty fetched Miss Lowen to meet Nelly. The lady in beige listened to Nelly sing *America the Beautiful,* a song Nelly frequently sang for school assemblies. Miss Lowen agreed that Nelly would be a wonderful addition to the choir.

Lily led Nelly into the front parlor. The room felt large, with its high ceilings and tall windows facing Henry Street. An upright piano stood in front of a collection of chairs arranged in three rows. Lily counted ten children sitting quietly. The rude girl, Edith, sat in the front row next to the piano. Lily also recognized Martha Gingham, Sasha Romanoff, and Fritz Shriver from school. They were in fifth and sixth-year classes. In the back row sat Joshua Cohen, wringing a black cap in his hands. Lily and Nelly joined him in the back row.

"Hi, Joshua," said Nelly.

"Ha-ha-hello," stuttered Joshua. He crumbled his cap

harder. "M-m-m-my pa-pa-papa said s-s-s-singing w-w-w-would be g-g-g-good," He took a breath, "for me." Joshua let out a long sigh. Nelly patted his shoulder and smiled. Joshua was always a likable boy, yet painful to talk to him.

"Of course it would," said Lily.

Edith turned her blonde head of bouncing curls and glared at the back row. Miss Lowen walked into the room, clapping her hands for attention. "Good afternoon, Choir. We have a lot to cover today, so let's begin."

Edith stood up, patted down her pale pink dress with a yellow ribbon trim around the waistline. "Miss Lowen, I can't imagine my Cousin Lillian tolerating a stammering child tripping over notes and words just because his father brings fabric and notions. Honestly, I thought you were serious about organizing a choir. Perhaps he should go home."

"Well Edith, I can imagine Miss Wald being extremely proud of Joshua's brave participation," said Miss Lowen. "His cantor has vouched for his beautiful voice and I am very pleased he is joining us."

Edith sat down with the huff. Lily could not understand what made this girl so mean. She patted Joshua's hand.

Miss Lowen led the group in vocal exercises; singing up and down the scales in different keys. Lily could feel her chest fill with musical air as all the voices melted together. Nelly sang clearly, and Joshua's voice was smooth. He closed his eyes and sang the notes up and down in rich tones.

Miss Lowen passed out song sheets. Lily knew there was a way to read the different shape notes within the five lines but did not know the code.

"Music is a universal language," said Miss Lowen. "The timing, notes, and key notations are interpreted the same way in every language. We can all count beats, move our voices into whole and minor spaces. The music in English, Italian, German and Russian operas is the same. We sing the notes in unison, as one community, lifting our hearts to music. The only difference is the words."

Lily's artist heart glowed. She was in the right place.

After forty minutes, choir practice ended. Lily and Nelly walked into the playground. Small children and Tony were playing *Freeze*. Tony was *It*. He looked like a giant among the little kids chasing, shouting, and tagging each other.

The carrot hair boy hobbled on his crutch and tagged Gigi, who stood frozen in mid-stride, mouth wide open.

"Thanks for melting me, Angus," said Gigi.

Gigi happily skipped to Lily's side and waved goodbye to her new friends.

"I like playing on the playground," said Gigi.

"Good," said Lily. She wanted to say that she loved singing in the choir, but, instead, she reminded Gigi with a stern look and voice, "You can't tell Mama and Papa." Her tone sounded like Margaret.

"I won't," said Gigi, "I promised God."

Edith stood by the entrance to the outside street. She whispered to another girl. Her green eyes fluttered as she stepped back and nodded toward Lily. Edith sneered as Lily, Gigi, Nelly, and Tony passed through. Lily heard her say to the other girl, "Honestly, I don't see how these dirty children are permitted inside the house. It will take all afternoon to get the stench out of the parlor."

Lily understood. Edith Reicher was just plain mean.

CHAPTER 21
SECRETS AND TEARS

Wednesday, May 31, 1911

THE PLAN WAS WORKING. Patty left a weekly order for two loaves of bread and a dozen Knot Surprises each Wednesday. It was fortunate that Miss Wald scheduled a political meeting on Wednesday nights.

"Men and women planning change. Miss Wald calls it reform," explained Patty. "Reform labor making safe places to work. Give women a voice and a fair wage and a means to keep their kids healthy. 'Dey argue and shout into the wee hours." Patty took a breath. "Did 'ya know Miss Wald got the school board to hire nurses makin' sure the kiddies grow up strong, not harboring disease? And did ya'know Mrs. Roosevelt, herself, the Senator's wife, has tea right here in me kitchen with Miss Wald. Fine lady, that Mrs. Roosevelt. She volunteered here at the Henry Street Settlement in the early days. Fine lady with a big heart, she be. Aye, the Henry Street Settlement do more 'den send nurses out to care for the sick 'n poor."

Lily nodded. She was astounded at the work Miss Wald

coordinated. Gigi tugged on Tony's arm. She pulled him out of the kitchen and led the way to the playground.

"And did ya' know Miss Wald and Miss Forsythe have babies and the mommy's come to learn about feeding and hygiene?" continued Patty. "Oh, such a sweet sight, fat happy cherubs!"

"Mama should come to baby school," said Lily, "Violet still cries a lot. The evaporated milk helps sometimes, but the Strega's oils and prayers never work."

"Wednesdays, noontime. Tell your mam," said Patty.

Lily knew Mama would never come. She would not understand so much English at one time, and she suspected those who were not Sicilian. To make matters worse, the news of children being snatched and held for ransom made Mama more fretful. She did not want to venture too far from Mott Street.

Papa warned Betta and Lily to keep Gigi close. "Hold Gigi's hand. Don't let her out of your sight. And don't talk to anyone you don't know."

"But I know everyone on Mott Street," said Lily, "You know everyone."

Papa said every day new faces appeared in the neighborhood. Sometimes it was hard to recognize the old faces who had grown desperate for food and money.

"Rocco Staducci got fired for signing with the union. He disappeared two weeks ago, leaving the wife with three hungry kids," reported Papa. "His wife got arrested for stealing a turnip! A turnip!"

"What will happen to her? What about the children?" asked Betta.

"I hear the government will send her and the oldest kid

back to Messina. The other two are Americana. They can live with family in Jersey," said Papa, chewing a squash slice.

Mama put down her fork and stared at her full plate. The real Mama would have shaken her fist, hollered at the injustice, and tell Papa to find out where the government held the woman and her children so she could bring fresh bread and a prayer. But this was the somber Mama with sad tears falling into her chipped plate. Violet shrilled in her basket. Mama walked into the front room and disappeared into Papa's chair, staring out the window.

Betta picked up the baby. "Shh. Shh, sweet Violet. Mama loves you. Papa loves you. Sisters love you."

Gigi snorted.

While Mama languished in her melancholy, Betta thrived. Miss Forsythe instructed Betta on how to prepare bottles and stroke Violet's tummy. She also made Betta take walks beyond the stoop. Now Betta was strong enough to walk with Tony to the Public Library nearby Seward Park. She thrilled at the sunshine and the leafy shadows dabbled on the sidewalks. Betta chatted with the lonely librarian and brought home two or three new books each week. She had to rest only one time on a park bench on the way home.

Nelly and Lily sang in the Henry Street Settlement House Children's Choir on Wednesday afternoons. Tony took Gigi to the playground to swing, jump in and out of long skipping ropes, and play tag. Gigi laughed and glowed. When it was time to go home, the little sister put her thumb in her mouth and left her joy on the playground. Tony and Lily took turns dragging her home.

Somehow Gigi remained true to her promise. She never talked about the playground, tag games, jump rope chants, or the shortcut through Seward Park. Like Mama, she barely talked at home. Lily felt guilty not being totally honest. She wondered if Margaret was right. Was she taking advantage of Mama's melancholy?

"I'm so proud of you, Gigi, keeping our secret," whispered Lily when the sisters nuzzled in their bedrolls. Gigi sucked her thumb and put her free hand over an ear. Violet was crying again. Pink rage ricocheted through the cramped three rooms.

"Bad baby," said Gigi.

CHAPTER 22
A FINE TREAT

Wednesday, June 14, 1911

MISS LOWEN ARRANGED the choir in voice order. Nelly sat in the front row with the other girls, who sang in a high register called sopranos. Edith took the front and center place. Her blonde curls bounced below a loose pale green bow that perfectly matched her dress. The hem fell to her ankles—a lady's length. Lily pulled at her skirt that could only reach below her knees. She sat in the second row Miss Lowen called the alto section. It was a slightly lower register that harmonized with the sopranos. Joshua took his place next to Lily. Three other boys sat in the third row—the tenors.

Miss Lowen walked into the parlor wearing the same plain beige dress. Lily thought it must be her Wednesday dress, or perhaps, her only dress. Mr. Horowitz followed behind, carrying a box with a large funnel. The box had a crank on the side and a metal bar on the top connected to the funnel. On the side of the box, Lily spied a metal tag with a stamp of a dog listening to the funnel.

"Thank you, Mr. Horowitz," said Miss Lowen.

"My pleasure, Miss Lowen," said Mr. Horowitz. He set the

box on a small table. "You kids are in for a fine treat." He adjusted the funnel. "This here part is called the star horn. Magic comes out of this star horn." He spotted Lily and sent her a wink, then left the room.

"There are several announcements today," said Miss Lowen. "Mr. Horowitz is correct. You are in for a fine treat! This, children, is a Victrola. It is a marvelous invention and—"

"Yes," said Edith, popping up to face the group, "My father donated this one since he bought the latest model just last month. He wants to be sure I continue to be inspired by the musical greats, for my acting career, you know, while I'm here doing good work with Cousin Lillian."

"Yes, Edith, we are grateful for your father's generous donation. And we are aware of your ambitions," said Miss Lowen.

The group was all too aware. Edith frequently mentioned her acting and singing experiences back in Rochester, her home city, the famous musicians she met, and the concerts she attended. Miss Lowen appeared patient. Sometimes one or two of the boys would quietly groan. Lily rolled her eyes.

Miss Lowen took a breath, then held up a black disc. "We call this a record. They somehow etch a recording of voices and music on the record. I crank the handle so the record may turn and place this needle on the arm on the record to play the music. The music is amplified through the star horn. What a marvelous invention! The great masters can now live forever."

Lily could feel her excitement.

"Children, we live in an amazing time," said Miss Lowen. She placed the record into the box and cranked the sidearm. The disc rotated. "Listen to the talented opera star, Louise Homer, sing *America The Beautiful*." Miss Lowen placed the metal bar that connected to the star horn on the edge of the rotating disc.

At first, Lily heard scratching sounds, but then a beautiful voice sang out of the horn. Lily knew the song. She sang it in school, but this Victrola record transported her to the majestic mountains, golden fields of grain, and shining seas!

"My, my," sighed Miss Lowen, "Miss Hammond's recording inspires pride in this beautiful country. Perhaps, one day, I will see those purple mountains and amber waves of grain." Lily nodded in agreement. Perhaps she may see those sights as well.

Miss Lowen passed out the music sheets. The choir practiced *America the Beautiful*. The sopranos led the melody as the altos and tenors brought in the harmony. Lily did not want to admit that Edith had a beautiful voice. However, when Edith tried to reach an octave higher at the end of the song, she fell flat. Miss Lowen played the correct note on the piano.

"Sing this part with your group, Edith," said Miss Lowen, "No need to show off."

"I'm not showing off, Miss Lowen," said Edith. "Singing is my talent, my gift! Obviously, you have no appreciation and cannot instruct properly." She slapped the music sheets on her seat and stormed out of the parlor.

This was not the first time Edith left choir practice in a huff. She believed she deserved special consideration because her father was a *philanthropist*. Lily was not sure what a philanthropist did but it sounded important. Miss Wald and Miss Lowen did not give in to Edith's demands. They treated everyone fairly and kindly. Once she cooled off, Edith would offer a half-hearted apology, as she always did, and blame her short temper on the hard work she was doing.

Miss Lowen blinked away the rude retort. "Well then, children, our dear friend, Edith, will miss the next bit of cheerful news." She waited for complete attention. "Children, we are invited to sing at the New York Highlanders Fourth of July baseball game at Hilltop Park!" The third row gasped. Miss Lowen almost danced on her toes. "We will start the game with *America The Beautiful*. Mr. Horowitz will play the accordion and I will conduct you." She clasped her hands together and grinned so wide Lily thought the corners of her mouth might touch her ears. "I do love a baseball game!"

Miss Lowen explained that the Henry Street Settlement Children's Choir will be the guest of the New York Highlanders. "We can watch the game for free and receive a voucher for a lemonade, a bag of popcorn and a hot dog!" The choir burst out in a standing applause.

"Miss Wald knows so many people," continued Miss Lowen. "She met Mr. Farrell, the owner of the Highlanders, who complained about the poor attendance. It seems that the Giants have a new field at the Polo Grounds, and the Brooklyn Trolley Dodgers have better viewing stands. Miss Wald suggested that a community choir performance would endear the fans to come to the ballpark, cheer on the team, and buy refreshments."

The group applauded. Joshua shouted, "Oh boy! Oh boy!" Everyone chatted with excitement as they returned the music sheets and left the parlor.

"Lily and Joshua, may I speak with you?" asked Miss Lowen. "I have another surprise, but I need to talk with both of you first." Miss Lowen tapped the music sheets into a neat pile.

"Mr. Farrell said that many spectators leave the field before the seventh inning so he can't make money selling Cracker Jack, beer, and ice cream. And it deflates the players' morale." She took a record out of a paper sleeve and placed it in the Victrola.

"Miss Wald suggested another idea. She has so many wonderful ideas." Miss Lowen gulped to catch her breath. "She proposed to select two children from the choir to sing a popular song. Their voices must be theatrical and powerful." Miss Lowen looked directly at Lily and began cranking the Victrola. "Miss Wald and I believe you, Lily and Joshua, can sing this song." She placed the bar on the rotating record. A man's voice sang the first verse through the scratches. Lily rocked on her toes as the catchy chorus rolled out—

> *Take Me Out to the Ballgame*
> *Take Me Out to the crowd*
> *Buy me some peanuts and Cracker Jack*
> *I don't care if I never get back*
> *For its root-root-root for—*

Miss Lowen picked up the bar. "We'll substitute Yankees for the words home team. The papers call the players Yankees and it fits better than Highlanders." She returned the arm to the record and let the song finish. It was a story about a girl who preferred to go to a ball game rather than see a show with her beau. The beat was jazzy, and the words gave the song excitement and fun.

Joshua blurted out, "Yes! Yes!"

Miss Lowen handed the music sheets to Lily and Joshua. "Joshua, you are the narrator and Lily, you will sing the Katie Casey's part. Study your parts. Practice your voice and breathing exercises. We need you loud and—"

"Powerful," said Lily.

"Yes, powerful," said Miss Lowen. "This will be a spirited performance!"

Lily watched Gigi swing back-and-forth, giggling and laughing with the carrot hair boy. She hummed *Take Me Out To The Ballgame* tune. Miss Lowen was right. The tune was fun and jazzy.

"I would not be surprised if all the spectators join you," said Miss Lowen. She explained that Lily and Joshua's powerful voices will ring through the field. "Singing on the

Fourth of July is a grand opportunity and who better to sing it than new American children?"

Lily's heart filled with joy as she hummed and rubbed the folded music sheet in her pinafore pocket. Joshua tapped Lily's arm. He looked more triumphant than when he solved long division problems.

"Sing the news to your papa," said Lily. Joshua nodded, then sprinted out of the playground.

Suddenly, Lily's heart deflated. Mama and Papa will have to know about the choir, Gigi swinging on the playground, and singing at Hilltop Park on the Fourth of July. She rubbed the music sheet again. The secret must come out.

CHAPTER 23
SCHEMES FOR PERMISSION

Thursday, June 15, 1911

LILY AND NELLY practiced their reasons to be allowed to sing at Hilltop Park with the Henry Street Settlement Children's Choir. Nelly was almost sure Nonna would give her permission, but she wanted to be absolutely sure Lily could go. They sat on the bottom step of the front stoop while Gigi drew patsy boxes on the sidewalk with a rock.

"It is a patriotic song," said Lily. "When we sing, everyone will stand up with their hands over their hearts."

"It's free," added Nelly, "We don't have to pay for a ticket, and we get lemonade and popcorn and a hot dog for free! Nonna would like that part."

"And we have to make sure we say that baseball is America's game. Every American loves baseball. Papa would like that part and he likes baseball." Lily looked out into the colorless street. She missed the vibrant colors of the playground on Henry Street and Seward Park. Hilltop Park probably burst in greens, blues, and reds. "Oh, Nelly, my heart just wants to sing!"

Nelly tossed her head toward Gigi. "What about the Gigi

problem? Your mama is very suspicious someone will snatch Gigi in the park, like the little Fantana boy. He disappeared while his aunt sat on the park bench, reading a book, and the little boy played on the swings."

Lily shook her head. "Mama cried and cried on her bed when she heard the little boy's family called the police after the Black Hand told them not to. They found his poor body in the trash can."

"Signora Bocchino told Nonna that the boy's aunt tried to hurt herself and she doesn't speak anymore. His mama goes to the cemetery every day and lies on the grave," whispered Nelly.

Lily looked over at Gigi. What would happen if someone kidnapped her younger sisters? Even though the little ones are difficult to care for, real Mama would chase a Black Hand down and fight, but this somber Mama may crumble in despair like the little boy's aunt and mother.

"Tony comes with us. He is our protector," said Lily, "And Henry Street playground is very safe."

Lily and Joshua practiced *Take Me Out To The Ballgame* in the bakery basement. Joshua sang his part with a strong and steady voice. He showed Lily how to stand facing the audience and hand expressions. His uncle Oscar, a Yiddish theater actor, gave Joshua tips in using his face and body to express the song into a show.

"When you sing the part, pretend you are shouting at imaginary umpires and the team," sang Joshua. His words came out smooth as silk.

The song told the story of a girl wanting to go to a baseball game instead of a date to Coney Island with her beau. Lily thought of Miss Smith and her beau, Jack Reynolds, who took her to a baseball game. Lily pretended to be a sweet young lady telling her imaginary gentleman she wanted peanuts and Cracker Jacks. The force of her voice grew louder when she sang *root-root-root- for the Yankees*. Mrs. Goldberg wildly applauded. Aaron drooped his shovel and joined the excitement.

"You dress in fine lady costume," said Mrs. Goldberg, "Then you shout, root-root-root! Ha-Ha!"

Lily hadn't thought about what she should wear. She would need a hat and gloves. She'd also need a dress. Her black Sunday dress, a hand-me-down from Margaret and Betta, was not a young ladies frock.

"First, permission," said Mrs. Goldberg, "Papa and Mama must say yes. Then we find fine lady costume."

"I promise. I am waiting for the right time. Nelly promised to ask Nonna when I have permission," said Lily. She was about to ask if Mrs. Goldberg had gloves or a hat she could borrow, but the woman twirled away toward her husband.

"Simon, we go to ball game. We root-root-root for Lily and Joshua," said Mrs. Goldberg.

"When such a game?" asked Mr. Goldberg, leaning on the bread paddle.

"It's on 'da Fourth of July. 'Da Yanks play a doubleheada'," said Donny, "Da' kids sing in 'da second game. I 'dink it starts at four."

Joshua held up his hand, wiggling his five fingers. "Five 'clock," said Donny.

"Important day this America birthday. Yes?" said Mrs. Goldberg.

"And who to watch shop on such important America birthday?" asked Mr. Goldberg, "Who to make coffee, sell bread?"

"Perhaps John and Donny stay, make coffee," said Mrs. Goldberg, turning to the boys.

"Awe, Mrs. Goldberg, we were gonna try to sneak- err- pay to get in to see 'da game," said Donny.

"And no one wants coffee on a hot July fourth afternoon," said John. "You could close in the afternoon."

Mr. Goldberg raised his right eyebrow. "We see, my Anca." He flashed her wink then returned pushing dough in the oven and pulling out golden brown rolls.

Mrs. Goldberg twirled back to Lily and Joshua. "Not to worry about Mr. Goldberg," she said. "Permission first."

CHAPTER 24
MEANIES AND BOSSY SISTERS

Thursday afternoon, June 15, 1911

DONNY ASKED Lily to deliver the afternoon rolls and bread to the Henry Street Settlement. He did not want to miss a chance to play stickball. Rumors buzzed that Curly Crisp was in town and he might show up in the Eldridge Street alley. Lily decided to quickly run the errand, then go home to ask Mama for permission. She would be sure to spend extra time with Gigi.

Edith was waiting in the Henry Street Settlement kitchen. She pretended to help Patty count out plates and silverware for the afternoon's political meeting. Edith threw open the kitchen door before Lily knocked twice.

"There you are!" she hissed, pulling the breadbasket from Lily's hands. "I knew you would find your way back to gloat."

Lily was not sure what gloat meant. She stood agape at the doorway.

"Don't set your heart on singing the duet with that stammering fool. What makes you think filthy street waifs deserve a spotlight when it is me who should have the part! I am a trained actress and have had voice and piano lessons since I was five years old. My father is an important benefactor to this little social project. He will see that I am not about to be upstaged by a little girl who stinks of garlic and sweat, and a half-wit boy. Immigrants, no less. Honestly!"

Patty called from the stove, "Is that you, Lily? Come in, lass. I have the bakery envelope for ya'." Lily grabbed the basket back and entered the kitchen. Edith stomped into the main house, her blonde curls bouncing off her shoulders.

"Don't you forget to bring the plates in now," called Patty. She returned to her wooden spoon and pot of stew. "That gal, a troubled one, she is. Fancy school kicked her out." Patty sipped the stew from the wooden spoon, then continued to stir. "Her parents be travelin' throughout Europe, don't 'ya know. Miss Wald agreed to take her in 'til July. God help us, tryin' to teach her a bit of humility and compassion. Heart of stone that gal."

"Is she really an actress?" asked Lily.

Patty turned and pointed her wooden spoon at Lily. Gravy dripped on the floor. "Twas a school stage she flits about on. Trouble, that gal. You and Joshua deserve to sing that special tune."

Lily ran all the way to the bakery. She wanted to get home before Gigi balked about being left out. A Thursday delivery to Henry Street Settlement was not the same as Wednesday's. Margaret counted the money from the envelope then marked the big book.

"Do you think Mama will give me permission to sing at the baseball game?" asked Lily.

Margaret closed the big book and sighed. "These days, Mama is scared of everything. And Papa doesn't want his daughters showing off. It's not our place."

Lily couldn't believe Margaret's words! Margaret was a

bossy 13-year-old Sicilian immigrant girl working in a Jewish Bakery. She kept track of money and inventory and could now continue to high school. Mr. Ross the principal was awarding her the Highest Honor Medal in front of the entire school. Everyone expected Margaret to do great things and take her place beyond the tenements and the factories. To Lily, Margaret was the biggest show-off on Mott Street. She told Margaret so.

"I'm not solving algebra problems or writing essays on stage for applause," said Margaret, slamming the cash register drawer closed. "My work is important. Practical. Not show-offy selfish."

Margaret didn't understand how music was important, too. She didn't see how music uplifted spirits and expressed feelings. Miss Lowen said since the dawn of man, music played. Through the ages, music inspired progress and enhanced beauty around us. Isn't that important, too? Humming tunes and belting out a performance with her powerful voice made Lily's heart soar. Lily wondered if long division made Margaret's heart sing.

CHAPTER 25
FEVERS AND MESSES

Friday afternoon, June 16, 1911

THE RAIN POURED down in sheets. Water flooded street gutters and pooled into a brown sludge from loose garbage and manure. Debris flowed down the street and sidewalks. Rumbles of thunder rolled in from the East River. Despite the rain, peddlers hawked their covered vegetables, oysters and fish for Friday night suppers. The milliner left his hat inventory at home and sold umbrellas from the corner. The newsie boys pulled damp evening papers from their oil bags.

Lily and Nelly leapt over puddles and dodged people in the same rush to get out of the rain. Lily carried the loaf of Daily Bread under her pinafore. It was just out of the oven, warm and inviting. Mrs. Goldberg sniffed the goodness before handing it over to Lily. "Ach, most beautiful."

Lily's shoes and stockings squished as she climbed the stairs.

She made up lyrics to the Take Me Out Ballgame song.

Take me out of this rainstorm
Take me out of the floods

Get me dry shoes and hot chocolate
I can't wait for the sun to come back
For it's one, two, three more steps up
To my warm dry home!

Nelly laughed.

"I'm asking Mama today," said Lily, "When I came home yesterday, Violet was crying and Gigi whined and whined to go outside. I couldn't talk to Mama before Papa came home. But today, I can't take Gigi out in the rain."

Violet's wails traveled to the third-floor landing. Lily and Nelly craned their necks upward, listening to the howls.

"Good luck," said Nelly, "If you get permission, come down, so I can ask Nonna." She waved goodbye to her friend.

Lily hurried. Mama was holding the bawling baby over her shoulder. Violet's knees bunched up to her chest, shaping her little body into a tight ball. She wore only a gray diaper and Mrs. Goldberg's booties; one orange the other blue with orange trim. Splatters of vomit and poop streaked Mama's apron—back and front. Betta stirred a wooden spoon in a boiling pot of water filled with baby gowns and diapers made from the Goldberg's flour sacks.

The rain pounded on the front room windows, trapping in the humid air. Mama's stray hairs hung in wet strings. Her rolled sleeves revealed puffy veins traveling up and down her arms and hands, covered by a clammy sheen. Betta's drench face tracked rows of sweat. She wiped her eyes and neck with a rag and stirred the pot of clothes. Gigi squirreled behind Papa's chair, sucking her thumb between sobs, perspired through her dress. The only thing that seemed to benefit from the trapped heat and dampness was the bodice of Margaret's Moving Up dress that hung in the front room. The pure white stood out in the dreary room.

Mama did not notice Lily walk into the kitchen.

"Poor Violet has been throwing up all afternoon," said

Betta. Lily put the Daily Bread on the table and quickly unhooked her shoes and stepped out of the wetness.

"Mama?" asked Lily.

"Betta, did the fennel tea cool?" asked Mama. Betta handed Mama a bottle filled with the pale green tea—Mama's remedy to settle headaches, upset stomachs, and the runs.

"Mama?" asked Lily again. Lily had not seen Mama move so quickly in such a long time.

"The Murphy kids are all sick with fevers and messes," muttered Mama to no one in rapid Sicilian, "The toilet is a hive of germs and cholera. This place is a death den. And the heat of summer has not begun yet!" Violet quieted and happily sucked down the fennel tea.

Mama handed Violet to Lily without looking at Lily.

"Mama?" asked Lily again. All the talking and activity seemed almost like real Mama, almost. Mama talked to herself and moved in frantic directions. This wasn't real Mama. This was scary Mama.

"I must clean, clean, clean the toilet closet. Now," continued Mama.

"You cleaned it earlier today," said Betta.

"Filthy Murphys contaminated it again," said Mama, "God knows what those Giordano brothers bring home, and the Durantes too." She gathered her bucket and rags.

Lily sighed and smiled at Violet. "Let's sit down, Violet." She will ask Mama later, after the cleaning.

Lily turned, still gazing at the baby. "When you are not bawling, you look like a pretty baby doll," whispered Lily. Lily took a step, but felt her foot bump, then tangle against her shoe. Lily held tight to Violet, but her foot tripped over the other shoe. Down she fell. Lily spun her body so she could land on her back, protecting Violet. The slip felt like hours of time, and all Lily could do was hold on to Violet and brace for the hard fall.

"Violet!" screeched Betta. Betta grabbed Violet from Lily's

arms. The baby whimpered when Betta pulled the bottle nibble from her mouth.

"She's ok, Mama," said Betta, "Lily, mind your shoes. You could have hurt Violet and broken your neck."

Lily wanted to argue that a broken neck was too dramatic when a bruise on her shoulder was more likely. She braced herself—prayed for a real Mama scolding. "Clumsy child!" Mama should shout, "Tripping over your shoes! Sloppy, thoughtless child!" Instead, Mama gritted her teeth.

"I am sorry, Mama," said Lily, getting up off the floor.

Mama sloshed boiled water into a bucket and added bleach. Wafts of the pungent smell filled the kitchen. Mama raked her hand through her hair. She darted her eyes around the room and grabbed the scrub brush. "I have to clean, clean away the disease." Scary Mama bolted out to the hallway to scour the toilet closet.

The real Mama would rattle her bucket and curse loudly so everyone on the floor would know about the disgusting messes people left behind. She would also add how Mr. Russo did not take care of the plumbing, and it was always up to her to fix something in the horrible closet. But this somber Mama grunted under her breath as she scrubbed, rinsed, and scrubbed again. The reek of the bleach seeped into the hallway, causing her to cough and sputter. Finally, Betta brought her into the apartment. Lily followed, carrying the bucket.

"Enough Mama, you got every germ," said Betta.

Mama washed her hands and arms with a lather of soap, pulled off her apron, and plunged it into the boiling water with diapers and baby gowns.

"Look Mama," said Lily, "Violet is sleeping in her basket." The baby's rosebud lips puckered as she breathed. A light line of yellow eyelashes trimmed her closed eyelids. Violet sighed in her sleep, content with her dreams.

Mama put her weary hand over Violet's little forehead. "No fever. Good. Good."

Mama looked so tired. Lily wondered how she was standing.

"Bring the basket and Gigi into the hallway. I have to clean everything. Germs are everywhere," said Mama.

Betta leaned on the wall, holding her head in her hand. "Mama, haven't we cleaned enough today?" Mama did not shout or slap her hand on the table. She dumped the bucket of dirty water and filled another pot. The facet rattled as it spit and coughed out the water.

"I'll help," said Lily. She picked up the basket and called Gigi. "Get up, little girl, I have a big sister job for you."

Gigi crawled out from behind Papa's chair, dragging Principessa with her. She rubbed her eyes and nose on a damp sleeve. "Can we play, now?"

"Not now," said Lily, "Follow me."

The three other tenement doors on the fourth floor were closed, but moaning, sharp arguments, sneezing and hacking coughs leaked behind each one. Twenty-seven people lived on the fourth floor, sharing the hallway and toilet closet. Lily lost count of the number of tenants living in the building. It was impossible not to hear each other's business or pollute each other's homes. Lily set the basket and Violet beside the thick banister.

"Watch Violet," said Lily to Gigi, "I will keep the door open, so we can see you."

"Violet's a bad baby," said Gigi. "She makes a mess. She makes Mama cry." Gigi's thumb returned to her mouth. Her mussed braids and stained pinafore from the day's grime and last night's supper showed the little girl was ignored as much as Lily felt.

"You were just like Violet when you were a baby," said Lily. "You always fussed and cried, and the messes you made were, you know, messy. But it didn't matter because I still loved you. I loved to sing to you and you smiled with no teeth! Margaret and Betta argued about who got to hold you. Violet is just like you. She will grow up and always be your little sister."

"Did Mama love me when I was a baby?" asked Gigi.

"She always loved you, even with all your bawling and messes."

Gigi loudly sucked on her thumb and hugged Principessa. She looked at Violet, sleeping soundly in her basket. "When will she be a good little sister?"

"Soon. Then you will have to fight with Betta to play with her."

Gigi shrugged. "Violet makes me crazy. She makes Mama crazy."

CHAPTER 26

STEALING LITTLE SISTERS

LILY TUCKED the back of her skirt to the front, creating a pantaloon. It helped to keep the skirt from getting tangled in her feet as she scrubbed the floor on her hands and knees. She and Betta moved Papa's chair to the middle of the front room and piled the sewing baskets on the couch. Betta grunted with each swipe. Lily sneezed at the dust and grime hiding in the corners. Perhaps Mama hadn't cleaned since Violet was born. The only sound from Mama was the squish of the rag plunging into the scalding water. Rain pounded on the windows.

Lily helped Betta pile chairs on top of the front room table. Suddenly, a piercing scream exploded from the hallway.

"Lily! Lily! Help!" screeched Gigi.

Mama scurried out from under the sink. Lily and Betta dropped the chairs. From the doorway, they found Gigi holding onto the leg of a man dressed in filthy tatters. His stringy hair hung down to his shoulders. A black scarf wrapped around his nose and mouth. He held Violet in one arm and tried to swat Gigi with the other, but the little girl held tight.

"He's stealing my baby sister! Mama!"

Betta screamed into her hands and Lily stood mute and frozen. The man looked like a thief robbing a bundle. Mama pushed Lily and Betta aside and stepped into the hallway.

"Put down my baby," she said. Her voice was loud and stern. Lily had almost forgotten the sound.

"Money. Give me money," croaked the man in Sicilian.

The neighbor, Widow Giorgio, peeked through the crack in her door, then slammed it shut.

Mama took a step closer and shouted with such force her anger roared off the walls—the real Mama way. "Put down my baby! Now!"

"Money!" The man held Violet over the banister. "I will drop it and kick this brat down the stairs." He shook his leg, but Gigi grabbed tighter. Her white knuckles locked on the man's leg.

Everything stood still, including Lily's heartbeat. Could he drop Violet and throw Gigi down the stairs? He was wobbly on his feet. His balance could easily waver. Violet and Gigi would—

Mama held up her hands. "Okay! Wait! I'll get you money."

Mama shoved Lily and Betta aside again and sprinted to her bedroom. Within seconds, she was in the hallway, holding up a gun. Lily had heard about this gun, but never saw it. Papa gave it to Mama when he worked night shifts on the docks after Gigi was born. Mama kept it in the top dresser drawer among rosary beads and her sister's letters. She never had to take it out of the drawer until today. It had a thick black handle and two barrels. It looked heavy. Mama held it up with two hands.

"Put my baby back in the basket," Mama's rage seethed through her eyes. Violet wiggled and winced. She will soon bust out a deafening cry. The man teetered.

"What are you going to do? Shoot me?" sneered the man. His voice was rough and smug. He held Violet higher over the banister. "A weak woman, like you, can't hold that gun up, and would never pull the trigger."

Mama pulled back the hammer of the gun. The click cracked through the thick air.

"I'm close enough to splatter your brains," said Mama. Violet winced again. Gigi clenched her eyes shut and held fast. "Put her back." Mama braced her stance and aimed at the man's head. The man stood still, darting his eyes to the stairs, the doors, and at Mama. Not a breath stirred, not a heartbeat. Finally, he pulled his arms into his chest. Violet cried, breathing in his fetid stench.

"Please, signora, please take pity," cried the man, dragging Gigi on his leg. He gently lay the baby in the basket. Gigi held on.

"Lily," called Mama, "Get Gigi. Betta, take the basket." Lily and Betta scrambled. Mama held up the gun and did not take her eyes off the man. Lily smelled the man's awful stink as she carried Gigi into their apartment and plopped her on the cot.

"Brave big sister," said Lily, then rushed back to the hallway. The man's scarf fell onto his neck, revealing a haggard face.

"You bum!" cried Mama.

"Please, please have pity. I have no choice."

"You are a bum! Stealing babies, from your own people. Shame! Shame!"

The man tried to make his way to climb up the stairs to the fifth floor. From there he could escape to the roof. But Mama held the gun up higher.

"You go down the stairs," shouted Mama. "Let everyone know. You are the bum who steals babies." She pointed the gun toward the stairs. "Go down!"

The man reluctantly took three steps down. Mama followed him. Widow Giorgio slipped out of her apartment and screamed in a high-pitched cackle, "Go away! Don't come back." Lily followed Mama down the steps. Mama hollered for all the tenement families to hear.

"This is The Black Hand thief! A bum! He tried to take my baby and hurt my little girl, but I catch him!" Mama followed him down, staying three steps behind and holding up the gun with two hands. "Go out into the streets where you belong."

Doors opened to see the commotion. The man sobbed his sorrys as he gripped the banister to keep from slipping down steps.

"Out! Out you go with garbage," hollered Nonna.

A raucous of jeers reverberated through the tenement. Lily had never seen so many opened doors and people spilling from their tight homes. Neighbors shook their fists and spit at the man. Mama continued to rage. Nonna followed, waving her heavy iron. Mr. Russo opened the front door to the rain and wet streets.

"Don't come back," warned Mr. Russo, "You have no home here."

He slammed the door. Mama lowered the gun to her side. Neighbors cheered. Nonna buried Mama into her enormous arms and chest. Lily picked up Nonna's iron, watching Mama heave all the sorrows and fears from her heart.

"You have the bravest and strongest mama in the neighborhood," said Nonna to Lily. Lily nodded in agreement. She wiped tears from her cheeks and took a breath. Was she holding her breath all this time?

The neighbors clapped for Mama. Mama turned to see the crowd that had gathered.

"He snatched my baby, and beat my little girl," she announced. "He was going to throw my daughters down the stairs. He wanted money. If I didn't give him money--."

More shouts erupted. Mr. Russo gently took the gun away from Mama.

"I'll bring it back. We will wait to see if the cops come with questions," he said.

Mama nodded. Mrs. Cznek handed Lily a small pail filled with a fragrant concoction of vegetables. "Halászlé—Hungarian fish stew," she said, hoisting her infant on her hip. Mr. Schneider offered Lily a bottle of beer. Lily tucked it under her arm and thanked the stout man.

Nonna took the iron from Lily. Mama wiped her eyes, racked back her stray hair, and started back up the stairs.

CHAPTER 27
REAL MAMA RETURNS

MAMA TALLIED an endless list of chores and shopping as she and Lily climbed the stairs.

"Papa will be home soon and will want his supper."

Lily held up Mrs. Cznek's pail. Mama smiled.

"Do we have to keep cleaning?" asked Lily.

"We did enough for today," said Mama.

Once inside their home, Lily locked and latched the door. Safe. Betta jumped from the cot, twisting a rag. Mama assured her the kidnapper will never come back.

"Thank God," sighed Betta, falling back to the cot.

Gigi sat on the couch wearing only her underwear. She held Violet, who wore just a diaper, on her outstretched legs. Her mussed braids hung over Violet's face. The baby squealed and attempted to bat at the ropes of hair.

"Watch, Mama," said Gigi, "Violet plays my funny face game." Gigi stuck her tongue out and made goo-goo words at Violet. The baby scrunched her tiny nose. Her blues stared intensely at Gigi's mouth and silly sounds. Finally, Violet's pink tongue tip peeked out of her rosebud lips. Gigi broke out in a hearty laugh, and Violet grinned back. Her arms waved at

Gigi's braids. Mama laughed too—another almost forgotten sound.

"You are a hero, Gigi," said Lily. "You saved Violet."

"Violet is my little sister," said Gigi with a shrug. "She makes me crazy, but I love her, anyway."

Margaret banged on the locked door while Gigi and Violet enjoyed a bath in the kitchen sink. Mama washed the girls with the last of the lavender soap she had made last summer. Lily scrubbed the kidnapper's stink out of their clothes. Betta breathlessly told the entire story while rainwater dripped off Margaret. Margaret listened with her mouth agape and a shallow puddle gathered around her feet.

Papa arrived home to a volley of news from the neighbors. Mr. Russo handed Papa the revolver. "No one talked to the police. Your wife and daughters are safe."

Lily heard Papa's heavy foot stomps race up the four flights. Papa stood at the doorway, astonished to see his serene family. Lily was combing Gigi's wet hair, Violet slept soundly in her basket on the kitchen table, and Betta sewed buttons in front of the window. Mama stirred Mrs. Cznek's Hungarian fish stew under a canopy of freshly washed baby dressing gowns, flour sack diapers, cleaning rags, and Gigi's dress and pinafore.

Mama recounted the afternoon from Violet throwing up, cleaning the toilet closet, to Gigi holding onto the horrible leg. Betta added how Mama held up the gun with two hands. Lily told about how Nonna came out with her iron and the neighbors cheering for Mama.

"Cesca, he could have dropped the baby," said Papa.

"He wouldn't," said Mama. "Such a coward. He knew I would kill him."

Papa examined the gun. "There are no bullets."

Mama looked at the empty cartridge, then to the clarity of Papa's sea-blue eyes. "I would have killed him, anyway,

Stefano." She held up her hands, raw from cleaning and washing. "With my two hands, I would have killed him!"

The family smiled at Mama's fury. Mama took a breath and tamed the rage.

"Margaret put the chairs around the table. Gigi, get the bowls and spoons. Betta can slice the Daily Bread. Lily, be careful and don't spill the stew! Wash your hands, Stefano. It is time to eat."

The real Mama burst with demands and expectations. Lily smiled. Home felt like home, again. Real Mama returned.

CHAPTER 28
GOSSIP AND TALL TALES

Saturday, June 17, 1911

LILY RAN ALL the way to the Christopoulos General Store on Eldridge Street. Papa gave her money to buy two cases of canning jars. Mama planned to make her jams and sell them to the Goldberg's bakery. The jam sweetens the Knot Surprises.

Lily darted carts, weaved around horse manure, people, and pools of black puddles. The humidity lingered, trapping the stench and heat in every breath. Her hair stuck out in all directions, and her clothes clung to her damp body. Perhaps Edith was right—everything and everyone stank in this neighborhood. No matter how hard she scrubbed behind her neck and under her arms and aired out her dress and stockings each night, the smell of grime and decay stuck. The weekly bath was never enough.

The real Mama was back ordering everyone about. She was trapped in a deep melancholy but now her words returned. . Mama paid attention to everything. Lily decided to ask Papa for permission. Today. He said he was coming home for lunch. Lily planned to wait for him at the stoop and ask for permission.

Lily panted for air when she arrived at the General Store. People milled about the barrels of grain, browsed jars and cans. She waited for Mrs. Christopoulos to finish with a customer. The stout woman folded a cutting of sea green cloth while talking to another woman.

"I heard the bum lives on Mott Street, spying out children to steal," hissed the customer.

"He was lucky Signora Taglia did not shoot him right where he stood," said Mrs. Christopoulos. "Imagine taking a baby, demanding money. A horrible crime. Thank God the baby and the sweet little girl were not hurt."

Another woman, covered in a black shawl, shouldered Lily away. "The neighborhood is going to the dogs," croaked the woman. "No decency. Too many people."

"That's true," said Mrs. Christopoulos, "I don't recognize half the people who come in and out of our store. So many look like criminals." Mrs. Christopoulos seemed to have forgotten about finishing the wrapping.

An old couple scurried to the conversation.

"Francesca fought the thug with her bare hands! A bear that woman," said the old woman.

"She chased him down seven flights of stairs," said a young woman holding a bag with one hand and a squirmy child in the other.

"How can she chase him down seven flights?" interrupted the old man. "The tallest tenement is five floors!"

"She tackled him down the stairs and beat him like an old rag," continued the young woman.

"Francesca Taglia ran that scoundrel into the streets carrying the baby in one hand and the little girl on her back," claimed the shawled woman.

A gossiping crowd surrounded Lily in lilts of Greek, Italian, and Yiddish. The story grew taller and louder as they interpreted for each other. No one seemed to recognize her as Lily Taglia, daughter of the brave Francesca Taglia and witness to the kidnapping. Of course, Mama bravely stood up to the kidnapper. Lily will never forget how breath and time stood still when the man held Violet over the banister. The echo of the gun click rang in Lily's head.

A firm grip pulled Lily from the blathering pack.

"You're Margaret's sister, Lena? Lydia?" It was Thea Christopoulos.

"Lily," said Lily, "Thanks for getting me out of there."

Thea let go of Lily's arm. Although 14 years old, Thea stood shoulder height to Lily. Her dark eyes looked up. Her thick black eyebrows darken her brown eyes. There was a fine trace of hair under a long straight nose and along a narrow jawline. Her hairline came close to the borders of the eyebrows. When she turned her head, Lily thought she looked like a hairy crow pondering her next move.

"Thanks again for getting me out of there," repeated Lily.

"Why are you here?" asked Thea.

"Oh, I almost forgot! I need two cases of canning jars. My mama is making jam for the Goldberg bakery. Papa is getting the strawberries from the exchange market uptown, today. Mrs. Goldberg puts jam in her Knot Surprises. It is so delicious. Have you—"

"Follow me," interrupted Thea, leading Lily to the back of the store. Shelves filled with cans of beans, bolts of material, and sacks of peanuts, sugar, and flour lined the back room. Thea pulled two cases of glass jars packed in crates. She handed one to Lily and carried the other to the front of the store.

Mr. Christopoulos loomed large over the cash register. He was as wide as he was tall. Thick jowls hung from his turned-down mouth. Mr. Christopoulos looked over his spectacles and smiled. Lily had never seen Mr. Christopoulos smile. It looked like a lot of work to pull up those fat jowls.

"Lily Taglia, right?" asked the big man.

Lily nodded. Mr. Christopoulos never spoke to Lily or anyone else. She had only seen him holler at his wife and daughter, argue with customers, and grunt faint greetings at old ladies. Thea spoke to her father in Greek. Mr. Christopoulos punched the cash register keys and pulled the lever with his meaty hands. Lily put the money on the counter for him to count. He pushed two nickels back to her.

"I'll help you carry the jars to the bakery," said Thea.

"I have to bring them home so Mama can make the jam. She—"

Again, Thea interrupted Lily. "I know. I know. She makes the jam for Goldberg's Knot Surprises. I heard."

Each girl carried a case of jars. The glass gently rattled, so they could not walk too fast. They dodged people, small children playing patsy on the sidewalk, and the clutter on the sides of the tenement buildings and stoops. Thea stopped at an alley. Two boys threw a ball at each other while two other boys ran between them. Garbage can covers laid at the feet of the throwers. The runners tried to tag a can cover before getting tagged by a thrower. "Safe! Got ya'!" they shouted.

"Petey, hold the ball with your fingertips so you can get some spin on it," shouted Thea. The boy nodded and threw the ball to his pal.

"Uh!" exclaimed Thea. "It's like talking to a wall! If they would just listen they could be pretty good ballplayers."

"Is it true Yanni plays on the Highlanders team? asked Lily. "And his name is Curly Crisp now?"

"Where did you hear that?"

"I saw a baseball card. Curly Crisp looks just like Yanni but—"

Thea hefted her case. "I suppose it's not much of a secret now. Yeah, Yanni is Curly Crisp. A reporter came around to talk with my father. He pretended not to understand the reporter, but my mother blabbed all the details."

"That's so keen! Have you seen him play at a baseball game?" asked Lily.

"My father was so angry at Yanni for changing his name, but my brother had no choice if he wanted to play. He had to change his Greek name to an American name. Now he's the best slugger on the team."

Thea smiled. It looked just as surprising as Mr. Christopoulos' smile.

"The Highlander's manager came to see Papa with Yanni last week. They talked for a long time, smoked cigars, drank and came out with their arms around their shoulders like they were brothers." Thea hefted the caseagain and leaned into Lily. "Those Yankees boys have a real chance to win the pennant this year."

"I'm singing with the Henry Street Settlement Choir on the 4th of July at Hilltop Park," said Lily. She was sorry she blurted it out since she did not have permission yet. She shrugged the thought away. Thea wouldn't gossip. Besides, today Lily Taglia was going to get permission.

CHAPTER 29
PRINCIPESSA GIGI

LILY WAITED for Papa on the side of the stoop. He promised to bring home strawberries by midday. Lily silently rehearsed how she was going to ask Papa for permission. First, she would tell him how handsome he looked and ask how his route was doing today, and if he knew how those Yanks were doing. She would tell him how lucky she felt to have such a wonderful, handsome Papa. Then she will explain how nice it was at Henry Street Settlement and that the nurses and Miss Wald care so much about children, and how the playground is safe, and they have a free choir for her to sing with. And then, the most exciting thing, she can sing at the Highlander's game on America's birthday!"

"Sing the song, Lily," called Gigi.

Lily barely paid attention to Gigi hopping into the rock-scraped patsy boxes on the sidewalk.

"I can't," said Lily, "I'm looking for Papa."

Gigi picked up the pebble with two feet in one box, then put her hands on her hips. "You know Lily, I am a hero, and you have to do what I say because I saved Violet."

"Just because you saved Violet does not make you Principessa Gigi and me your servant."

Mama fussed over Gigi that morning. She spread extra butter on Gigi's toast and sprinkled sugar on top. She hugged the little girl, fussed with her pinafore, and braided her hair into long brown ropes. When Mama kissed the top of Gigi's smooth head, Gigi glowed.

"Besides, you didn't save Violet because you wanted to be a hero. You saved her because she is your little sister and you love her," said Lily.

Gigi stuck her tongue out at Lily, then tossed the pebble on the patsy board. The pebble rolled away. Gigi picked it up and gently placed it in a box.

Lily stretched on her toes, searching for Papa in the mass of people, carts, horses, and motor cars.

"Brave! Brava!," shouted Signore Costa. He came off the congested street, pointing a crooked finger at Gigi. "I knew this child would amount to something." Gigi smiled at the old man. "Yes, yes, she held onto that scoundrel's leg and wouldn't let him take the baby." He patted Gigi's head and melted back into the crowd.

"Thank you," shouted Gigi. "See that, Lily, the neighborhood knows I am a brave hero. I should be Principessa Gigi."

Suddenly Papa came out of the masses. Lily immediately recognized the tall man with red hair peeking out of his grey cap. He walked with a long stride around the carts and children carrying baskets, shouting peddlers and stooped women examining potatoes. His smile assured Lily that he was in a good mood, but his arms were empty. Where were the strawberries?

Before Lily could shout for his attention, Papa scooped Gigi in his arms. Gigi held his neck and smugly smiled at Lily.

"Come upstairs," he called to Lily, "I have news. Good news!"

Lily dawdled as Papa leapt up the stairs, and Gigi screeched with glee.

"*Amunnini* ! Lily, Let's go!" he called.

When Lily reached the fourth floor, the Taglia's door was wide open. Happy squeals and laughter seeped into the hallway. Papa picked up Mama and twirled her around in the kitchen.

"Stop! Stop, Steffy," said Mama, "Put me down, you silly man." Mama tried to hide her joy, but her eyes danced and laughter came out of her mouth. Mama had not laughed in such a long time. Margaret and Betta were also laughing. Gigi clapped and danced on her toes. Even Violet giggled from her basket.

"What is everyone so happy about?" asked Lily. Yesterday, the apartment was eerily quiet, recovering from the horrible kidnapping.

"Oh, it's wonderful," said Betta. "Tomorrow, we're going for a drive in the country. Mr. Carter is letting Papa borrow the truck. Instead of getting strawberries from the market, we're going to drive out to Long Island and pick bushels of strawberries at a farm so Mama could make her jam."

"Oh, Stefano, I want to feel the earth again," said Mama.

CHAPTER 30
A FRIEND ON THE STRAWBERRY FARM

Sunday, June 18, 1911

PAPA PULLED Mr. Carter's motor truck in front of 125 Mott Street just as the day dawned. Mama carried Violet bundled in a crocheted blanket. A pale pink bonnet Mama knitted the night before crowned the baby's head. Lily handed a bag filled with diapers, clean rags and two cans of evaporated milk to Tony, who stood in the truck bed. Betta carried a netted grocery bag with their picnic lunch; bread, cheese and a thermos of tea and another thermos with cold caponata—Papa's favorite eggplant dish.

Betta, Mama, and Violet rode in the front with Papa. Gigi, Tony, Nelly, and Lily piled into the open back with stacks of peck baskets. Margaret stayed behind to work in the bakery and finish hand-stitching her Moving-up dress. Nonna promised to mark the hem to Margaret's height in the afternoon.

"My hands must stay as clean as possible," said Margaret, holding up her hands. I don't want to get smudges on the white material."

Lily knew better. Margaret did not like walking about

muddy fields. She preferred concrete blocks and cobblestone streets where she can see a pile of manure and puddles before walking through them. Dirt, manure, and grime were all over the farm. Lily could not wait to run, touch, and smell the Earth. She wouldn't mind a little dirt in her fingernails.

It was a bumpy ride out of New York City, over the Brooklyn Bridge and into Huntington, a village on the north shore of Long Island. Lily and Nelly took turns holding Gigi down so she would not bounce out of the bed truck. Finally, Papa pulled onto a dirt road. More bounces and rumbles, then a full stop next to a small cottage. Paint peeled from its sides, revealing its worn age.

Papa pushed the truck door open, got out, and stretched his long legs. He put his hands on his hips and took a deep breath.

"We're here!"

Here was a wide field filled with straight and even rows of low-lying greens and ruby dots. The scent of strawberries filled the air.

The door of the cottage creaked open. A Negro man ducked his head so as not to hit the top of the doorway and walked out sideways to fit through. Lily recognized Sam, Papa's partner, when they worked the docks. Lily had seen Sam one time on the night of the horrible fight that almost killed Papa.

Sam stood a head taller than Papa and his skin was black as pitch. He wore faded overalls over a white collared shirt.

"Morning, Stevie," he called, waving a letter in the air, "I gots your letter."

"Good to see you, Sam," said Papa, reaching his out to shake the big man's hand.

Sam pulled Papa in and wrapped his long arms around him. He lifted Papa off his feet.

"Ain't Sam no more," said the big man, patting Papa on the shoulder. "Go by Jeremiah, Jeremiah Jones; Jerry for short.

Keepin' that city life far behind me. I'll go by another name come winter when I follow the picking harvest south."

Jerry explained he joined a group of migrant workers. "We is all poor folk plowin' 'nd harvestin'."

He lived in barracks with several men and some families. Women and kids worked just as much as the men. They move from farm to farm depending on the needed jobs. Since that horrible night when Jerry brought Papa home beaten and bloody, he had worked on three farms—one in Queens and the others on Long Island. The Huntington boss liked Jerry right away. Jerry was strong as a mule, and could read and write and figure sums.

"Funny how my folks mind this ugly giant reading off the day's work order over listening to a proper white boss. One of these days, I gotta write my teacher, Miss Juniper. I brought her to the edge of insanity in teaching me. Good woman. Never beat on one child. She say beatin' a child only make him angry, not smart."

Lily thought Miss Triptree could learn a lesson or two from this Miss Juniper.

Jerry looked over at the Taglia family. "Why shoot, Stevie, you sure do have a nice-looking family." He pointed his thick, black finger at Lily. Gigi tightly held Lily's hand. "I 'member you. You done thank me. Brave young gal you got here, Stevie."

Lily smiled and shook Gigi's hand. It felt good to get a little recognition.

Jerry told them that the rain ruined this patch of strawberries. "Bossman say ain't fit to market and factories ain't got no call now. Bossman be a good friend of your Mr. Carter and Mr. Carter say your wife make jam and sell to the bakery so he make deal."

Papa handed a roll of bills to Jerry. "Here's the money for your boss," said Papa. "It was lucky your boss hired you. It's hard to trust people I don't know."

"Don't I know it," said Jerry, shoving the money into his pocket, "Bossman say he will tell Mr. Carter if he got overripe peaches, pears, and blueberries. Better sell something then get nothing."

"Blueberries are my favorite," said Lily.

"You all come August 'nd gather up all the blues that ain't fit for market," said Jerry. "Maybe I see ya' then. I gotta get on back. Sunday prayin' day. I gots me a woman makin' sure I pray on Sunday."

Jerry waved good-bye and walked down a dirt road. Mama looked at the wet ground and told the children to take off their shoes and stockings. Everyone took a peck basket and started out into the strawberry field. The hard rain swelled the berries. Some had rot spots.

"We can cut those black spots out," said Mama, "Be gentle. Don't squeeze."

Lily tasted a soft berry. A burst of sweetness popped in her mouth. She wiped juice dripping from her chin. The ground was muddy and slick. Gigi fell twice and came up with mud pasted on her pinafore. Her face was covered with a mix of mud and strawberries. The cool earth and the scents and tastes of strawberries made Lily forget about the smelly city streets. The sun warmed the clean air.

Papa sang his favorite song from his village, Ciuri Ciuri (Flowers Flowers). His robust voice moved Lily to join the song three rows away. Nelly's voice mingled in as well. Their voices melded in harmony, surrounded by strawberry sweetness.

"Mama and Papa are in a good mood," said Lily to Nelly, "I'll ask for permission when we get home."

By noontime, the family had picked enough strawberries to fill the baskets. They sat on an oil cloth next to the cottage. Papa said it was a tool shed, not a home. Lily thought it was bigger than their home on Mott Street. Wouldn't it be grand to live in a shed on a strawberry farm?

They ate bread and cheese, even though their stomachs were full of strawberries. Tony walked into the nearby woods while everyone rested. Gigi and Violet napped next to Papa who gently snored with his cap over his face. Betta read a book and Mama crocheted. Nelly and Lily lay on the ground encircled with strawberries.

Tony trudged back with a handful of bright wildflower flowers. He held them out to Mama. "For, you, Zia. I am so happy to see you well again."

"Sweet boy," said Mama, accepting the wildflowers and smelling their beauty.

That night, the Taglia home smelled like the strawberry farm; sweet and earthy. Lily and Tony made several trips, gently carrying the baskets to the fourth floor so as not to bruise the delicate fruit. It was a lot of work, but the strawberries made Lily feel light and happy.

Margaret was in a great mood, too. Her dress was finished and it fit perfectly. Nonna pinned the hem and Margaret finished the hand sewing. She drew a vine and roses on a paper bag to model an embroidery pattern on the collar. The pretty dress hung in the kitchen over the cot.

Mama directed and demanded. She insisted everyone needed a bath. Water boiled. Lily helped Betta move the cot and dress to the front room and pushed the big tub in place. Mama washed Violet in the sink and Margaret scrubbed Lily and Gigi in the tub. Mama, Margaret, and Betta took turns in the bath. Papa got in the tub while the sisters cozy up in their bedroll in the front room. Before drifting off to sleep, Lily hummed Ciuri Ciuri. She noticed a daisy in Betta's hair.

It was such a busy happy day. Lily did not get a chance to ask for permission. Tomorrow will be the day. Absolutely tomorrow.

CHAPTER 31
THE STRAWBERRY ACCIDENT

Monday afternoon, June 19, 1911

THE TAGLIA HOME was a flurry of strawberry activity. Mama stirred a big pot of strawberries. Another pot filled with jars of strawberry jams simmered. Steam surrounded Mama, curling her loose hair, making her eyes shimmer with sweet delight. Pink stains streaked her apron. Gigi sat on the kitchen floor, leaning her head over Violet in her basket. The baby happily squealed and batted her arms at Gigi's braids. A milk bottle half-filled with water and Tony's flowers displayed on the shelf over the stove.

Lily placed her Daily Bread, and a bag of jars Mrs. Goldberg had given her on the table

"Good, you are home," said Betta. "You can shuck these strawberries, so I can take my walk. I've been cooped up here all day."

"Take money to buy potatoes and an onion. If escarole looks good, buy it," said Mama to Betta. "I'll cook it with the sausage I bought today." She pointed the wooden spoon at Betta. "And be sure the potatoes are firm."

Betta flung her apron at Lily. "Okay, okay!" and closed the door behind her.

"Gigi, take Violet to the front room," said Mama, "You make too much noise in here."

"Can I have a strawberry with sugar on top?" asked Gigi.

"Not now. You had some at lunch. After supper."

"But I want it now," whined Gigi.

Mama slapped the wooden spoon on the table, startling the cooling jars and Lily. She pointed the stained spoon at Gigi. "I said no! Do what I say. Take Violet to the front room."

Gigi pouted as she pushed Violet in the basket. Lily sat at the kitchen table and cut the strawberry tops and cores with a small knife. It felt good to have real Mama back—loud, demanding, and in charge.

"Don't squeeze the strawberries. They are overripe."

Lily nodded. "Mama?"

"And be sure to cut out the spots."

"Okay, but Mama?"

"Doesn't Mrs. Goldberg have more jars? I'll need more jars."

"I don't know but—"

"Crazy woman, probably put them somewhere she can't remember."

Lily sighed. How was she going to ask for permission when Mama kept interrupting? She talked and talked. Perhaps she was making up for all the lost time when she was quiet and sad.

"I will need sugar, too," continued Mama, "And I want to buy thread. The thread Margaret chose to embroider the roses is not the right shade of red. It is too dark. It needs to be brighter. Margaret thinks she knows how to pick colors but she picked a dark red as if it were the dead of winter. Her dress needs a brighter shade for summer and for an important occasion. Lily, watch what you're doing."

A knock at the door interrupted Mama. Lily opened the door to Miss Forsythe.

"Hello Lily, is your mother home? Oh, what smells so delicious?"

Miss Forsythe put her black bag on a chair and hung her cape and hat on the wall peg.

"Hello Miss Forsythe," said Mama's in English, "I make jam, the berry jam. Err, Lily, how you say?"

Lily held up a mushy strawberry. "Strawberry."

"Yes, strawberry. You want cafe, tea?" Mama's English was improving. The family spoke Sicilian in their home, but when Miss Forsythe visited, Mama practiced English.

"Oh no, thank you. It is much too hot for coffee or tea," said Miss Forsythe. "How are you, Mrs. Taglia? I heard about the horrible kidnapping attempt. How terrifying. Are you well after such an ordeal?"

Mama smiled in the steam. "Good. I drove the bum out. No more hurt. No more take babies. See Violet."

"Alright then, I'll check on the baby," said Miss Forsythe. She grabbed her bag and walked into the front room. She stopped to admire Margaret's dress hanging on the wall. "Lovely. Margaret will look beautiful in this dress! And here is our hero, big sister Gigi!"

Lily heard Miss Forsythe exclaim how brave Gigi had been and how big Violet was getting.

"Lily, put some strawberries in a bowl and sprinkle a little sugar on top," said Mama. "Bring it to the nurse."

Lily sighed. She will never get to ask for permission this afternoon with all this work. Why does she have to do everything?

Lily filled a small bowl of shucked strawberries and sprinkled a spoonful of sugar on top. Juices pooled a shallow puddle in the bowl. She walked into the front room. Something caught under her shoe. Lily shook her foot but lost her balance. The bowl of strawberries flew out of her hands.

Lily fell to her knees. She looked up to see strawberries splattered on the wall where Margaret's white dress hung. Pink juice sprayed on the front of the bodice and dripped down the skirt to the floor.

For a very long minute, Lily did not move. She did not hear Miss Forsythe gasp or Gigi scream or see Mama standing with the wooden spoon dripping with cooked strawberries. Strawberry stains were harder to remove from fine cloth than blood.

Lily hid her face on the floor and cried, "I'm sorry. I'm sorry. What have I done?"

Miss Forsythe helped Lily to her feet. Gigi stood wide-eyed next to Violet's basket. Mama held the wooden spoon at the dress.

"Margaret is going to kill me," sobbed Lily, "Mama, I'm sorry."

Lily sat on the couch and buried her head in her hands. Her sobs heaved at her heart. She braced herself for a volley of insults and a wooden spoon beating. Lily will admit that she was a clumsy child, an ungrateful child. But Mama just looked at the dress holding up the wooden spoon.

"Stop, Lily," said Mama in English, "We fix. Miss Forsythe, you help, too."

CHAPTER 32
A STRAWBERRY DRESS FOR MARGARET

Mama took over. First, she wiped the dripping strawberry juice from the dress. Pink stains streamed from the bodice to the hem. Mama handed Miss Forsythe rags and then lifted jars with the canning fork from the pot of boiling water.

"Catch it," she ordered Miss Forsythe.

"Margaret's going to kill me," sobbed Lily as she wiped down the jars.

"No, dear," said Miss Forsythe, "Margaret will understand it was an accident."

"I tripped on something," continued Lily, "I didn't mean to ruin Margaret's dress. I am so sorry."

Mama slapped the table with her hand, startling Lily from her tears. "Basta! Enough crying," said Mama. She grabbed Lily's face and looked directly into a pool of blue. "It happened. We can't fix it with tears and sorrys."

Mama released Lily and kissed the top of her head.

"You are my good girl." Lily's heart fell to her stomach. Through all of Mama's sad times, she did notice Lily's helpful deeds. Despite the tripping, stalling, and clumsy sewing, Mama said she was her good girl. Lily suddenly felt terribly guilty at trying to take advantage of Mama's melancholy.

Mama wrung out a clean rag and handed it to Gigi, who was standing along the kitchen wall clutching Principessa. Gigi quickly hid the doll behind her back.

"Clean up the strawberries from the floor and watch Violet," said Mama.

Gigi went right to work without a whine or peep of protest.

Betta walked in carrying a paper bag with escarole leaves poking out. Mama did not give her a chance to gasp or say hello to Miss Forsythe.

"Make a bottle for Violet and have Gigi feed her. We need your help," said Mama.

Soon the jam was ladled into clean jars and set into a pot of simmering water. Mama washed out the jam pot, then filled it with clean water and a stream of salt.

"I put dress in boiling saltwater," said Mama to Miss Forsythe.

"Will you add bleach to get the stain out?" asked Miss Forsythe.

"No. Berry stain too deep," said Mama, "Bleach break fabric. We color dress with strawberries."

"A strawberry pink dress!" exclaimed Miss Forsythe, "Signora Taglia, you are a wonder solving this problem so quickly."

Mama shrugged, stirring the salty pot, "Women job."

Betta and Lily shucked and cut a bowl full of strawberries while Margaret's dress boiled in the saltwater. Mama pushed the strawberries through a meshed strainer.

"See?" said Mama, "Summer pink color."

Lily nodded. Perhaps this wasn't such a disaster. Margaret liked pink. She will love a pink dress. Lily could only hope.

Margaret walked in just as Mama and Miss Forsythe finished twisting water from the dress. Lily started to cry again.

"What have you done!" shouted Margaret. She grabbed

the dress and whipped out the twist, spraying warm water on Lily and Miss Forsythe. Margaret screamed at the faded pink tracks dripping down from the front of the dress.

"Who did this?" she demanded.

"Now Margaret, calm yourself. It was an accident," said Miss Forsythe.

Margaret sputtered in Sicilian and Mama shouted back. Lily cried into her hands. She was wrong to think this was not a disaster. She ruined the dress and Margaret would never forgive her.

Margaret pulled Lily up and shook her shoulders. "You did this!"

"I'm sorry," blurted Lily. She hung her head down so as not to see the fury in Margaret's eyes. "I didn't mean it. I tripped. I tripped on something."

"You clumsy, selfish little kid!" shouted Margaret, "After all I do for you, you ruined the one thing I can have for myself."

Violet and Gigi cried from the front room. Miss Forsythe slipped in to comfort them.

"It was an accident, Margaret," repeated Mama. "We can fix it."

Margaret let go of Lily's shoulders with a jerk. "You are a silly little kid, Lily, who thinks only of herself. So stupid of me to help you and keep your secrets."

"Please, Margaret, please don't."

Margaret turned to Mama.

"Mama, your little songbird is a dishonest sneak," said Margaret pointing an accusing finger at Lily. "She's not just delivering bread on Wednesday afternoons."

Miss Forsythe walked into the kitchen carrying Violet. Gigi hid behind her grey skirt.

"Oh Margaret, please. This is for Lily to—"

Margaret ignored Miss Forsythe.

"This snotty songbird sings in the Henry Street Settlement Choir while Gigi plays on the playground. But that was not enough. Now Lily got herself picked to sing at the baseball park in front of a field of people. She has been scheming on how to disobey Papa and take advantage of your melancholy to get permission. She is so fixed to do what she wants, she doesn't pay attention to what is important."

Lily buried her face in her hands. Margaret spoke the truth. She was selfish and clumsy and didn't pay attention. Papa will be disappointed, and Mama will never say she was a good girl.

Margaret huffed and leaned into Lily's covered face. Lily felt the heated rage.

"Stupid me for keeping her secrets and covering for her. She thanks me by ruining my dress—the dress I made by myself, with Connie's fabric. You're the worst sister!"

Margaret stormed past Miss Forsythe and plopped into Papa's chair. She turned away from everyone and stared out the window.

Lily's heart broke into a million pieces as she cried harder. Margaret was right. She ruined everything. Papa will be disappointed, Mama will never trust her, and Margaret did not want to be her sister.

Mama took Violet from Miss Forsythe.

"Thank you for come."

"Please, Signora. Gigi was never in danger and Lily is a wonderful girl, so helpful. She is just a child with a playful heart."

"Thank you for come," repeated Mama. She handed Violet to Betta, who was cowering in the corner.

Miss Forsythe retrieved her black bag, spoke softly to Margaret in the front room, then left.

Mama handed Lily the bag of potatoes and escarole.

"Take the food and Gigi to Nonna. Wash and cut up the vegetables and wait there."

Lily continued to sob as Gigi led her to the third floor. Nonna gathered Lily in her thick arms. Nelly, relieved to tell

Nonna about the choir, explained everything as Lily rocked in Nonna's embrace. Gigi recounted the strawberry accident.

"They hate me. They will hate me forever," said Lily. "I'm a terrible sister and daughter. I don't deserve my family."

"No, no, cara mia," said Nonna, "Only an accident. Only mistake was not being honest."

"Will they send me away?" asked Lily. "Or will they make me stay at home always and never go to school or the bakery? Will I be allowed to go to the stoop?"

"Will they send me away, too?" asked Gigi.

"Why?" asked Nonna. "What have you done?"

Gigi clutched Principessa to her chest. Tears welled in her dark eyes.

"Because it was my fault," said Gigi in a quiet voice. "I left Principessa on the floor and Lily tripped on her. It was my fault Margaret's dress has strawberry stains."

"No one will go away," said Nonna. "Promise." It was unnecessary for Nonna to swear to God promise because everyone knew Nonna was always true to her words.

Lily and Nelly quietly peeled and cut potatoes. Gigi ripped escarole leaves while Nonna finished the day's pressing. They could hear Mama and Margaret's voices leak from upstairs. Nelly held Lily's hand when they heard Papa clomp his feet up the stairs. Another wave of tears came over Lily. Gigi hugged Lily's arm. A loud commotion of sharp voices seeped from Nonna's ceiling.

CHAPTER 33
RUINED DREAMS

Wednesday, June 21, 1911

IT HAD BEEN two days since the strawberry accident. Lily pretended to listen to Miss Triptree read the Public Library invitation for children to apply for their library cards and borrow books over the summer. Lily could not pay attention. In her mind, she worried. Her family hated her. What was to become of her?

Lily was told to go to school and bake Daily Bread at the bakery. She had to come home after school and watch Gigi play on the front stoop. They could see Mama feeding Violet and watching from the fourth-floor window. Lily didn't dare move from the last step.

Mama snapped orders for Lily to set the table, fetch coal, and fold laundry. Papa said nothing about the strawberry accident, the Henry Street Settlement, the playground, or singing at the Highlander's baseball game. Margaret avoided looking at Lily. She seethed when she had to tell Lily to hang diapers on the roof and to mind Gigi and Violet while she, Mama and Nonna, talked with low voices. Lily was convinced they were planning on never allowing her beyond the front stoop.

Even though Betta was home with Mama all day and whispered to Lily at night, she did not know what was to become of Lily. Lily felt like a caged bird. Unlike a caged bird, Lily would never sing again.

~

Lily thought back to that awful strawberry accident. Memories of pink and strawberries dripping from Margaret's snow-white dress haunted her mind. That night, Tony brought ice chips. Mama left the dress in the pot of strawberry juice, vinegar, and ice chips overnight. On Tuesday morning, Mama rinsed the dress, wrung out the water and hung it above the cot next to the stove.

"Look!" said Mama to Margaret, "Your dress is a pretty pink shade. You cannot see the stain lines."

Papa nodded his approval. "I like the strawberry pink better than white."

Margaret looked over the seams and pulled the skirt out, searching for the stain tracks. The dye colored the dress evenly. A slight smile came across Margaret's face but quickly disappeared when she spied Lily watching her.

Now it was Wednesday, and no one mentioned singing or the baseball game. Another well of tears brimmed her eyes. Perhaps she should surrender to the fact her heart will never sing again.

Mr. Crandall threw down his baton. "Lily, where is your voice today? I don't hear the rockets. You'll ruin the Moving Up ceremony!"

Lily wanted to tell him her heart was too sad, but she just held back her tears in silence. Everything was ruined because of her.

Only Mrs. Goldberg understood Lily's melancholy. On

Tuesday morning, she wrapped Lily in a warm embrace and hummed their favorite tune—the theme to Sleeping Beauty in the Woods. Lily breathed in the coffee and vanilla scents on Mrs. Goldberg's apron, but she still felt she was the cause of the disaster. Tuesday's Daily Bread was as heavy and lumpy as Mita's.

∿

Finally, the school day ended. In two days, school would end for the summer. Nelly listed all the things they could do together during the long days.

"Maybe we can take a trolley uptown, see the fancy shop windows, and the lions and tigers at Central Park! Wouldn't it be grand to sing to the beasts?" Nelly carried the basket of bread and Knot Surprises to deliver to the Henry Street Settlement. She and Tony were to deliver the basket, then come right home.

Lily could not tell her friend that she would probably be in tenement prison all summer. She will have to sew, mind Gigi and Violet, and clean from morning to night. She might not be allowed to bake Daily Bread anymore or walk beyond the front stoop.

Gigi ran up to Nelly and Lily from the front stoop. She grabbed Lily's hand and pulled. "Come on, Lily. Let's go!"

"Where?" asked Lily.

"To the playground. It's Wednesday. I swing. You sing. Remember?"

"I'm not allowed Gigi," said Lily, "We are not allowed."

Betta was waiting on the top of the stoop. It was a warm bright afternoon and Betta looked like a shining princess in the midst of busy and noisy Mott Street. Betta skipped down the steps. Her long red braid bounced and her blue eyes sparkled.

"Mama said to deliver the basket with Tony and Nelly,"

said Betta, "Bring Gigi, too." She took the Daily Bread from Lily's arms. "Oh my, it's heavy, again."

"Where's Mama?" asked Lily.

"Out with Nonna and Violet," said Betta, "I have to finish some sewing before I start supper."

"Let's run," said Gigi, pulling Lily's hand when they reached Seward Park.

"There is no rush, Gigi," said Lily. "I am not singing in the choir and you are not swinging on the playground." Her voice caught a sob. Nelly put her arm around Lily's shoulders.

"I'm sorry I ruined your chance to sing as well, Nelly," said Lily, "I should have been honest and asked Mama and Papa right away."

CHAPTER 34
MAMA ON HENRY STREET

EDITH OPENED the door to the Henry Street Settlement kitchen.

"There you are!" said Edith, grabbing the basket. "It seems our little bird has fallen. Miss Lowen finally came to her senses." Edith tossed her blond head, swaying her perfect curls. "I will sing solo at the ballgame. Honestly, street waif, you and that stuttering fool have no place on a stage."

She was about to shut the door when Tony held up his arm to stop the slam. Edith's eyes narrowed into an angry glare.

"Release the door, you hoodlum," hissed Edith.

Tony gritted teeth. "The bakery needs to be paid."

Edith shook her blonde head and lifted her chin. "Certainly. Wait there. Keep your stink outside so as not to infect our supper."

"You are mean," shouted Gigi.

"And you are a sniveling immigrant," snapped Edith, slamming the door.

Gigi stomped her foot, then kicked the door. She took a deep breath and kicked harder. Patty opened the door.

"There you are, darlin's. I see the basket on the table but no sweet faces about."

"Edith is a meanie," declared Gigi.

"That she is, lass," said Patty, "Come along. Your Mam and Granny be sitting in the yard with Miss Wald."

Lily stood frozen in the middle of the kitchen. "Mama is here?"

"Nonna, too?" said Nelly.

Patty took Gigi's hand and led the way to the playground. Lily heard the echo of the choir singing scales in the parlor. Her heart ached. A wave of tears brimmed in her eyes.

Children ran, skipped rope, and laughed in the yard. In the corner, surrounded by purple wisteria and vines, Mama and Nonna sat on wrought-iron chairs with Miss Wald. Mama held Violet on her lap. Both Mama and Nonna wore their black Sunday dresses and a shawl across their shoulders.

Gigi bounded to Mama's side. "Mama, watch me on the scuper. I can swing by myself."

Gigi scurried to the middle scupper, noticed her friend, Angus, sitting motionless on a swing seat, then quickly slipped off. She gave Angus a push and scooted back to her place.

"Watch, Mama!"

Gigi flew up and back, squealing with joy. Mama smiled and turned back to Miss Wald.

"As you can see, the yard is very safe for children," said Miss Wald, "The Henry Street Settlement is here for everyone in the neighborhood."

Tony started to interpret, but Mama held up her hand. "I understand," she said in English. She turned back to Miss Wald and stood up. "I talk to husband."

"Of course," said Miss Wald, holding out her hand to shake Mama's hand. Mama hefted Violet and nodded her head. Lily wanted to hide from the embarrassment. Why couldn't Mama learn American customs like everyone else?

Miss Wald smiled in a friendly way. "Your husband is welcomed at any time."

Nelly helped Nonna to her feet. Mama told Lily to get Gigi. It was time to go home.

"I want to swing some more," whined Gigi, "Go sing, Lily."

"We have to go," said Lily, pulling Gigi off the scupper.

"Can we come back?" asked Gigi.

"I don't know," said Lily. She looked over at Mama waiting by the street gate, adjusting Violet's bonnet. Nelly and Nonna had started for home.

Lily felt sick. She wiped a tear away before it fell down her cheek.

"Not fair! I want to swing. I want to play," said Gigi, stamping her feet.

"You make me crazy!" snapped Lily, shaking Gigi's hand. "Swinging on scupers is not important."

"Swinging is important," said Gigi. "The swings make me happy. It's important to me just like singing is important to you. It's the same."

Lily looked down at her little sister. The twin braids hung in front of her pinafore and her big brown eyes looked up at Lily. Gigi wiped a drip of snot from her nose and stuck her thumb in her mouth.

It didn't matter that Lily had an artist's heart and a powerful voice. She was poor, a daughter of immigrants living in the Lower East Side tenements. Survival depended upon each daughter working hard and doing what was expected. One mistake, one sneaky deed could lead the family into disaster. There would be no forgiveness. There was no room for dreams in the crowded streets and tiny apartments. It was silly of Lily to dream. She did not belong in the Henry Street Settlement Children's Choir or deserve to sing at the baseball game. Only girls like Edith can dream. The sooner Gigi learned this lesson, the better off she will be.

CHAPTER 35
MOVING UP MORNING

Friday, June 23, 1911

MARGARET BURST through the door and held up her dress. Her head full of curling rags shook with anticipated excitement. "Look! Nonna pressed the pleats perfectly and see how evenly the strawberry dye worked through?"

Margaret propped the dress against her body. The sailor collar laid flat across the bodice and the skirt fell in soft pink pleats to her ankles. Margaret kept the dress at Nonna's home, away from clumsy sisters. This was the first time Lily had seen the dress since the strawberry accident. "Oh the color is so pretty, Margaret," exclaimed Betta. "It is so becoming on you."

"Help me," said Margaret to Betta. The girls rushed into the front room.

Lily thought that perhaps this was a good time to ask what was to become of her.

Since Wednesday afternoon, Mama only ordered Lily to fetch coal, wash diapers, and fold laundry. Betta and Gigi did not have any news to share with Lily and Margaret avoided her. Papa looked at Lily with disappointment. Now it was

Friday, the last day of school and Moving Up was at five o'clock in the afternoon. It should be an exciting happy day, but Lily's heart felt heavy with guilt. No one noticed how sorry she was and promised to never be dishonest, again—swear to God promise.

"Mama?" squeaked Lily.

"Wash out the baby's bottle before you go to the bakery," said Mama.

"Alright, Mama," said Lily, "But I wanted to know—"

Margaret walked into the kitchen wearing her dress. Betta followed behind, patting down the back of the skirt. Papa stood up and beamed at Margaret. She did look beautiful, even with the curling rags hanging off her head. The pink brought out a glow to Margaret's olive complexion and a shine in her dark eyes.

"Bedda! You are beautiful Margherita," said Papa. He kissed Margaret on both cheeks, "You make me so proud," He patted his chest and looked down at his shirt. "I hope I don't pop my buttons at Moving Up." Margaret glowed. Lily couldn't remember the last time Papa kissed her.

Mama examined the fall of the skirt and how straight the seams around the neckline and sleeves lay. "This is fine work, Margaret. And the embroidery around the cuffs and collar is lovely." She held Margaret's hands and nodded her approval. "I am so pleased." She leaned in and kissed Margaret's cheeks. Margaret's eyes brimmed with tears of happiness.

Lily's heart dropped. Will she ever make Papa proud and Mama pleased?

CHAPTER 36
MOVING UP AND ROCKETS

Friday night, June 23, 1911

THE AUDITORIUM AIR hung thick and stale. Children and parents filled the room with chatter and damp and smelly odors from unwashed clothes and dirty bodies. Paper fans fluttered and handkerchiefs wiped sweaty faces. Necks stretched and arms waved at the eighth-year students sitting in three straight rows on the stage.

Margaret sat in the middle of the front row. She looked forward out into the audience. Her long black curls hung down her back. A big rosy pink ribbon held the sides of her hair to the back of her head. Mama bought Margaret white stocking to wear with the strawberry dress. The skirt draped across her lap and touched her ankles. Lily saw Margaret glowed strawberry pink, standing out against the grey and white backdrop of her classmates. She even seemed to outshine Agnes Harrigan, the prettiest girl in the school.

Lily sat with the music class in the front row of the auditorium. She pulled at the hem of her Sunday dress. Mama nor Betta had time to let out the hem or extend the cuffs since her arms and legs grew so long. Even her black stockings pulled up too short. Betta brushed out Lily's copper-red hair, weaved one thick braid and tied it with a scrap of white ribbon.

Lily turned toward the crowd and craned her neck. Papa borrowed Mr. Carter's truck to bring the family to the Moving Up ceremony. Margaret rode in the cab between Papa and Nonna. Mama, carrying Violet, Tony, Betta, Gigi, Nelly, and Lily, bounced in the back of the truck through the neighborhood and into the school lot. Although Betta could not attend classes, she passed her exams so that she could move up with Tony to the seventh year.

Lily spotted her family and the Goldberg's in the middle of the audience. Gigi sat on Papa's lap, and Mrs. Goldberg sat next to Mama, cooing and singing to Violet in her arms. Betta and Tony flanked Nonna, who leaned into her seat, wiping her face with an embroidered handkerchief. Everyone was there to see Margaret move up and out of elementary school in pink glory.

Finally, Principal Ross invited everyone to stand for the *Pledge of Allegiance*. The audience rumbled to their feet, placed their right hands on their hearts, and recited the promise. While everyone sat back down, the music class walked to the front of the stage. Lily pulled at her dress. Mr. Crandall played the introduction to the *Star-Spangled Banner* on the piano. He mouthed toward Lily, "Ready!" Lily nodded and the class sang.

Lily's voice mingled in harmony with the group. She could hear Nelly and Joshua's smooth voices. Lily felt tears well up in her eyes. She hadn't sung or hummed a note all week since the strawberry accident. Her artist heart loosened. The music escalated. She sucked in a deep breath and opened her mouth. Lily's heart swelled and her voice belted out glaring rockets through the auditorium and out the doors. Mr. Crandall banged out his approval on the piano, so relieved Lily found her powerful voice. Lily looked out and saw Papa and Mrs. Goldberg pop out of their seats. The audience roared with applause. Papa shouted, "Brava! Brava!" Mrs. Goldberg looked like she wanted to twirl to the front of the stage and pick Lily up. Principal Ross pumped his arms up and down, trying to calm the ruckus. Mr. Crandall slid to the side of the music class and waved his arm.

"Bow, children, bow to thank them," he whispered.

Lily and the class bowed to the applause. Mr. Crandall moved next to Lily and directed his hands toward her. The applause grew louder. Lily crossed her right foot in front of her left and dipped a shallow curtsy. Papa, Betta, and Mrs. Goldberg towered over the crowd, clapping furiously. Lily could not see if Mama was standing or clapping.

Finally, the audience took their seats, and the ceremony commenced. Big John received the Spelling B prize, Thea Christopoulos won the fastest runner medal for girls, and Mr. Crandall gave the music honors to Agnes Harrigan. Margaret accepted the civic, geography, math, art, home economics, essay, and recitation awards. Principal Ross announced Margaret was PS 24 1911 Valedictorian, an amazing feat for an immigrant girl. Margaret stood in front of the podium, proudly shaking Mr. Ross' hand.

CHAPTER 37
SEWING THROUGH RUINED DREAMS

Monday, June 25, 1911

SUMMER MEANT LONG, hot days on the city streets. Kids flooded the alleys and sidewalks, dodging shoppers and peddlers. They tried to play tag, skip rope or shoot marbles. Shouts, screeches, and bellowing voices hung in the thick air. The tenement windows, left wide open, allowed sultry breezes into the sweltering apartments. There was no escape from the heat, noise, and trapped smells of the Lower East Side. Lily felt there was no escape from Mama's anger.

Margaret's dress hung on the side of the wardrobe in the front room. Its bright color cheered the grey space. After mixing and setting her Daily Bread to rise in the bakery, Lily returned home to endure a day of sewing cuff buttons. She sat in a chair next to the open window. Hot air breathed onto her work. Lily hated sewing buttons.

"You must line up each stitch," instructed Mama. "Put the needle through the same hole."

Mama complained that Lily's buttons were too tight or too loose. She frequently ripped out Lily's work and impatiently demsonstrated again how to do the job right.

"The factory won't pay for sloppy work," said Mama.

"Sewing buttons takes practice," said Betta, "You'll get it."

Lily shook her head. "Mama hates me and everything I do."

By mid-morning, Betta's basket was full of finished collars and button cuffs. Lily's small basket was barely half full and her fingers ached from the needle pricks.

"Sing Violet the spider song, Lily. I forgot the words," said Gigi.

"Yes, we haven't heard you sing or hum at home in such a long while," said Betta.

"I forgot the words," said Lily. The needle stabbed her finger again.

Lily also forgot the words to the songs she made up for dough mixing, kneading and sweeping the bakery basement floor. Her artist heart did not completely mend at the Moving Up ceremony. Since that day, Margaret no longer scowled at Lily. Papa boasted that he was so full of pride, he popped two shirt buttons. One button was for Margaret's achievements and the other for hearing Lily's beautiful voice sing. But Mama barked orders at Lily and condemned her sewing. Lily was doomed to spend the stifling summer sewing cuff buttons.

Nelly burst through the Taglia store and plopped Lily's Daily Bread on the kitchen table.

"Quiet child," said Mama, "Violet is napping."

"Sorry, Zia," said Nelly, "Can I talk to Lily just for a minute?"

Mama nodded. Lily looked up from her buttons.

"Nonna said yes," whispered Nelly, "She'll let me sing in the choir and at the ballgame."

Lily smiled weakly at her friend. Betta put down her work.

"Nonna said she felt so proud when we sang at the Moving Up ceremony," said Nelly, a little louder. "But I won't go unless you are there, Lily. I can't sing with heart and pride without you."

Lily lowered her head. Once again tears fell.

∾

The heat hung like a thick wall on Tuesday afternoon. The bakery shop held little reprieve. Even beautiful Mrs. Goldberg sweated, her damp tendrils stuck to the side of her face. Despite her discomfort, she always had a smile for customers who stopped in for an ice tea and a conversation.

The ice man came every day to deliver a block. Aaron chipped the ice block. Mrs. Goldberg wrapped a chip in a headscarf and wore it around her neck. She made one for Lily, but Lily barely noticed the heat. Her thoughts sat empty, and her heart was broken in a million pieces.

Since Lily stopped singing at the bakery, Mita filled the empty air space with her constant talking. She had a comment about the heat, the spoiled meat her aunt bought, how sick the old rabbi's wife was, and how terrible Joshua felt about losing his part to sing *Take Me Out To The Ballgame*. Lily tried not to listen. More tears welled up. Lily could not believe her eyes produced another flood of tears. She did believe that her artist heart will never mend.

Mama let Lily take Gigi to the Henry Street Settlement and deliver a special bakery order for an important political meeting and gave in to Gigi's plea to let her play in the yard.

"Fifteen minutes and Lily must be in the yard with you. Come right home," said Mama.

Gigi ran to her friends. Lily sat by herself, leaning on her fists while watching happy children skip rope. The street gate opened to Edith and another girl strolling into the yard. Edith's blonde curls were tied high off of her neck. She wore a light yellow dress, straw hat, white kid gloves, and carried a blue parasol. Lily hated to admit how pretty Edith looked— prettier than Agnes Harrigan.

Edith nodded toward Lily, then whispered to her friend. The friend looked over at Lily and shared a giggle with Edith.

Lily grabbed Gigi's hand. "We have to go home."

Gigi spotted Edith and did not argue.

"She's an ugly girl," said Gigi loud enough for Edith to turn her head, "I don't like her."

"I don't like her either," said Lily.

Lily and Gigi stopped in front of the General Store alley. Donny stood at the far end, holding a stick. Thea crouched behind him, her back against the slatted fence, holding a large brown glove. A tall man wearing a baseball cap called out to Donny.

"Put your left foot out and bend your knees, Donny boy," he called, "Elbows up higher."

Donny adjusted his stance and the tall man threw the ball. The stick slapped the ball and sent it past the man and onto the sidewalk. Lily stopped the ball from rolling into the gutter with her foot.

"Throw it here," called the tall man. He took off his cap and wiped his forehead. Lily recognized Yanni Chistopoulos! His hair was cut short but a tuft of black curls hung to his thick eyebrows. Lily tossed the ball to Yanni.

"Did you see that Yanni!" called Donny running up, "I mean Curly, Curly Crisp, star Yankee Highlander teaching me to hit a ball. Donny's droopy right side of his face almost smiled as broadly as his left side.

"Turns out, you're better off as a southpaw," said Curly.

He turned to Lily. "Hey, are you Margaret's little sister?"

Lily nodded.

"And me too," said Gigi.

"I hear ya' gonna sing at the game on the fourth."

Lily shook her head. "No, I don't have permission." Another piece of her heart broke.

"Too bad," said Curly, "I hear ya' got a powerful set of pipes."

Thea shouted from the back of the alley, "It's my turn! Hurry up before Papa finds us out here."

Curly turned away from Thea and cupped his hand to his mouth. "My sista' got a powerful set of pipes, too. Too bad she can't sing a note."

Lily and Gigi spotted Papa's delivery truck parked across the street from their tenement. Betta sat on the tailgate. Bushel baskets of leafy vegetables filled the truck bed.

"Papa brought fresh broccoli rabe home," said Betta. "I'm watching the truck for him. Papa said you should go upstairs, Lily. Principessa Gigi, you stay with me."

Lily climbed the stairs quickly, not minding the stuffy air amid the smell of rotting food and grime. She heard Mama shouting from the third floor. Papa's voice boomed when Lily reached her front door. He quickly opened the door without seeing Lily and shouted back inside the apartment.

"She can go, Cesca! I am the man of the house and I say she can go."

Papa looked down at Lily. His blue eyes danced with fury. Papa raked his wide hand through his red hair and placed this cap on his head.

"You sing in the choir and sing at the ball game. I, your Papa, give you permission."

"Thank you, Papa," squeaked Lily, "But Mama-"

"I want my Songbird back," said Papa, "I miss you." He stomped down the stairs.

Lily took a breath of hot, stale air and felt a small piece of her heart mend.

CHAPTER 38
MENDING THE HEART

Wednesday, June 28, 1911

LILY HUMMED while she sewed buttons as carefully as possible. Betta smiled at her and nodded her approval. Mama examined Lily's work and ripped out only two buttons.

Lily saw Mama was angry. Papa made a decision she did not like. She banged wooden spoons on the pot harder and grunted and humphed while mending and cleaning the floor. She ordered Lily to hang wet laundry on the roof, fetch coal, peel potatoes, and wash the windows with vinegar. Lily jumped at each order and anticipated Mama's needs throughout the hot morning. Despite the cloud, Lily's heartfelt lighter and brimmed with songs to fill the stuffy air. Gigi hummed along (out-of-tune) while they folded diapers and cleaned baby bottles.

It was a relief to knead and shape Daily Bread at midday, even though the bakery basement felt as hot as Dragon. Lily sang the theme to *Sleeping Beauty in the Woods*, and Mrs. Goldberg twirled and leapt across the basement floor.

At three-thirty, Lily skipped all the way to Henry Street, carrying the breadbasket. Nelly and Tony held Gigi's hand as they walked down the streets and through the park. The heat, crowds, smells, and noise could not dampen Lily's spirits. Joshua almost burst with joy when he saw Lily walk into the parlor.

"G-g-glad to s-s-see you," he stammered.

Lily patted his hand. She was glad to be there.

Miss Lowen directed the choir to sing scales in different keys. Edith shrilled at the high notes. Miss Lowen told her to take a deep breath, but Edith shook her blond curls and just huffed.

"Honestly, how can anyone breathe in this fetid air?"

The choir sang *America the Beautiful* in harmony. Miss Lowen beamed. Lily's heart swelled with pride. She was a little disappointed she would not sing Take Me Out to the Ballgame with Joshua. Edith had the solo, and there was no taking it back. Lily reasoned she deserved it since she was not honest with Mama.

CHAPTER 39
MITA'S NEWS

Friday, June 30, 1911

THE TINY ROUND buttons were almost impossible to sew onto a delicate cuff.

"These buttons make me crazy," said Lily.

"Like me," giggled Gigi.

Gigi played *Peek-A-Boo* with Violet. She draped a clean diaper over Violet's head and called, "Where's the baby?"

Violet moved her little arms up and down and squealed with delight until the diaper fell off her face. Gigi clapped and repeated the game. Lily wished she could play Peek-A-Boo on this hot Friday afternoon, but the sweatshop expected the collars finished before 3:00. Mama and Betta's baskets were almost full, but Lily's pile barely covered the bottom of her basket.

"Don't pull so tight," suggested Betta.

"Is this one okay, Mama?" Lily stretched to show Mama the buttons on the white cuff. Mama glanced, then looked into Lily's blue eyes.

"Okay," she said.

Mama got up from her chair, lifted Violet from the baby

basket, and walked into the kitchen. Gigi scrambled to her feet and followed, asking, "Mama, can I feed Violet?"

"Mama is still mad at me," said Lily to Betta.

"She's mad at everyone," said Betta, re-threading her needle. "She's mad at you, me, Papa, Margaret, Nonna, Mr. Russso, the scissor man. The list goes on."

Betta sighed. "She's especially angry living in the tenements. Papa says one day we will have a house with rooms for all of us, a yard with a swing, and a garden. One day, then maybe mama will be happy."

A rapid knock at the door broke Lily's attention. A button dropped and rolled somewhere under the couch.

Mita Cohen's voice came through the rooms. "Excuse me, Mrs. Taglia, I need to speak to Lily right away."

Lily and Betta put down their work and entered the kitchen. Mita was flushed with news and exertion. Joshua stood beside his sister, holding his cap in both hands.

"Lily! Lily!," gasped Mita, "Wonderful news. Incredible news."

Joshua rocked on his toes. His broad smile took up his entire face.

"I just can't believe it," continued Mita, "It is that marvelous."

"What is it?" asked Betta.

"Just marvelously grand," huffed Mita.

Mama handed the girl a glass of water.

"Oh, thank you, Mrs. Taglia." Mita took a sip. Everyone watched her swallow.

"Mita, what is it?" cried Lily.

"You just won't believe it," said Mita. She took another sip and placed the glass on the table.

"Miss Lowen came to the bakery," started Mita. "I was sitting with my friends, having a glass of iced tea before going home after kneading my Daily Bread. You know my friends are fascinated with how I bake bread for the family and keep up with all of my chores and studies."

"The news, Mita!" said Lily. Now she appreciated Margaret's impatience with Mita's rambling.

"Yes, yes. Miss Lowen came to the bakery, so hot and flustered. She did not want to sit and have a cup of iced tea to refresh herself."

Joshua pulled Mita's arm, imploring her to get the news out. "S-S-Say it-t-t."

"Yes, yes." Mita took a breath. "She was looking for you, Lily. It seems that the high-and-mighty Edith Richter was sent back home to Rochester. I heard that kind Miss Wald, her benevolent guardian while her parents were away in Europe, had enough of her stuck-up attitude and disobedience. You saw how she walked about with airs, believing herself too good to aid the poor and learn about Miss Wald's good work."

Mita took another sip of water. Mama drew closer. Joshua's smile somehow grew broader.

"What tip scales was that—," Mita cupped her hand to the side of her mouth and lowered her voice, "she went out on a date with a married man. She dolled herself up with rouge and he took her to a—" Mita looked at Gigi who was mesmerized by the story. "He took her to a B-A-R."

"Che?" asked Mama, growing as impatient as everyone else.

"Bar, Mrs. Taglia," whispered Mita, "A saloon."

Joshua pulled at Mita's arm. "T-t-t-tell n-n-n-now!"

"Yes, yes," said Mita. "Well, Edith's parents had just returned to Rochester after their trip and expected to see Edith at the ballgame on the Fourth of July. But once they heard of her foolishness, they took the first train and fetched the girl. They took her right back to Rochester. I suspect kicking and screaming. Even her indulgent father wouldn't tolerate such wretched behavior."

"What about the ballgame?" asked Betta.

"Well, that's the good news," said Mita. "She is not permitted to sing in the choir. I mean how could she. She is in Rochester!"

"You-You-You and me," blurted Joshua. He stepped in front of his sister and started to sing in a smooth, clear voice.

Take me out to the ballgame
Take me out to the crowd

Lily joined him. They belted out the song loud enough for the whole tenement to hear. Mama looked amazed.

CHAPTER 40
A STRAWBERRY DRESS FOR LILY

THE NEXT FEW DAYS WHIRLED. Despite the heat, Lily laundered, sewed buttons on collars (actually Betta sewed and placed collars in Lily's basket), washed floors, delivered bread, and swept the bakery basement floor. She did not give Mama a reason to scold or complain. Still, Mama said nothing about the baseball game or how Lily's voice brought cheer into the gray household. At midday, after Lily kneaded and shaped her Daily Bread, Mrs. Goldberg had Joshua and Lily practice their routine. She showed them how to bow and curtsy gracefully.

"Must show audience grateful for applause," said Mrs. Goldberg.

Joshua and Lily practiced each afternoon with Miss Lowen. Lily could feel her voice growing stronger from the breathing and scale exercises.

"This will be a sensational performance," said Miss Lowen, "We must discuss your costumes. You should look like a grown-up couple. What will you wear?"

"I have a s-s-suit, "said Joshua. "Uncle Oscar has a straw hat I can borrow and s-s-spats." Each day Joshua's speech improved.

"That is perfect, Joshua," said Miss Lowen. "Lily, how about you?"

Lily was embarrassed to say that she only had a black Sunday dress. Perhaps she could borrow Betta's dress. It was also black, but Betta sewed a white crochet collar and added white cuffs.

"I have a dress," said Lily, "And a hat too."

Lily raced home. There had to be something she could wear for the baseball game. Lily, Betta, and Nelly stared into the wardrobe. Pinafores, a green child dress Gigi had outgrown, and varying lengths of black and brown skirts and worn blouses hung from the pole. Lily took out her Sunday dress and examined the hem. There was barely a half-inch of material-not enough to let the hem down.

"I wish you weren't so tall," said Nelly, "then you could borrow my spring flower frock."

"I need the skirt to reach my ankles, like young ladies," said Lily. "Your dress would fall to my knees."

Margaret came in from the kitchen and closed the wardrobe doors.

"I have a perfect dress for you," said Margaret. She reached to the side of the wardrobe and unhooked the strawberry dress. She held it against Lily's body.

"The length is perfect, but we'll have to take in the bodice and waist a bit," said Margaret.

Lily's eyes welled with tears—happy tears. Betta snapped her fingers and pulled the couch from the wall. She dragged a crate to the middle of the floor and dug in until she found a blue cardboard hatbox.

"Mrs. Cznek traded this for a bunch of doilies I crochet for her. She did not come to America with her wedding linens." Betta pulled out a golden brown straw hat. She fluffed up the paper flowers and straightened the brim. "Mr. Cznek was a milliner in Hungary. Mrs. Cznek has other hats. I thought this one would be nice to wear to the park or library on a summer day."

"It would be perfect for an afternoon at the ballgame," said Nelly.

Betta placed the hat on Lily's head. Margaret held the dress up again.

"Well, something has to be done about your hair," said Margaret, "I wonder if we can borrow gloves."

"Thank you, Margaret," said Lily, "You are the best sister."

"No," said Margaret, "You are."

CHAPTER 41
PLEADING FOR FORGIVENESS

Tuesday, July 4, 1911

LILY ROSE from her bedroll before dawn. Papa dipped a slice of Daily Bread in his coffee while Mama rinsed boiled eggs.

"Today is the big day, Songbird. Are you ready to sing your heart out?"

Lily hugged Papa around his thick neck and kissed his cheek.

"There, there," said Papa, "No time for mushy kisses. Tell me again how you will get to Hilltop Park."

Lily took a step back and tapped her left index finger. "I will mix Daily Bread early this morning, come home, finish sewing my button quota, then go back to the bakery to knead and shape the bread before midday. That way the dough can rise sooner and Mr. Goldberg can bake it earlier."

Lily tapped her middle finger. "Then I'll come right home for Betta to fix my hair and pack the strawberry dress, stockings, and straw hat in a paper bag."

She took a breath and tapped her ring finger. "I will walk to Henry Street with Joshua and Nelly, practice, and change into the strawberry dress." Lily stopped to think. She did not miss a step.

She tapped her pinky. "The game starts at five o'clock. Mr. Horwitz will drive me and Joshua with Miss Lowen to the baseball game. Joshua's Papa will pick up Nelly and a few other kids in his motor car. Everyone else has a way to Hilltop Park."

Lily held up her left hand. "And the Goldbergs are closing the shop early. They will drop off my Daily Bread then take a trolly to the game."

"Mr. Carter is letting me off early today. I can use the truck to take Nonna, Tony, Betta, Margaret, and Gigi."

"No Gigi," said Mama, waving her wooden spoon. "It is too dangerous for a small child. Gigi stays home with me."

Lily's heart deflated. She had hoped Mama would soften. After all, Margaret forgave her. But Mama was stubborn. She will hate Lily forever.

"Come, Mama," said Papa in a quiet voice, "There is no danger if there are so many of us holding onto Gigi, and Violet, too. We should all go. It is America's birthday. Let's celebrate at American game and see Lily sing."

"I have work to do," said Mama, "There is no time for nonsense in the middle of the week."

Mama was still angry at Papa for giving Lily permission. Papa left for work, leaving Lily alone with Mama.

"I am sorry, Mama, I am sorry I did not ask for permission. But you were sick, and I could not talk to you."

Mama stepped in front of Lily, gripping the wooden spoon. Her dark eyes seethed as she looked into Lily's blue eyes. "You were a sneak and risked Gigi just so you could sing. You took advantage, made my troubles an excuse to sneak around, put Gigi in danger, and hold secrets. A selfish daughter."

Tears fell down Lily's cheek. "I'm sorry. I said I was sorry. How many times do I have to say it?"

"You go. Go to the baseball park. Sing. Sing for strangers. Your Papa allows you. It doesn't matter what I say."

Lily covered her eyes with her hands. Tears spread all over her face. She felt Mama's hot breath puff on the back of her hands.

"I know I am not your best daughter. Betta can sew and crochet and take care of Violet, Margaret does everything perfectly, and Gigi is brave. But I don't do anything right. I'm clumsy, and don't clean or sew good enough."

Lily wiped the tears from her face and took a fresh breath. Mama's head hung down. Was she crying, too?

"My dream is for you to be proud of me. I want you to see that I can do something well," said Lily without a sob. "I can sing, Mama. Please, Mama, come see me sing."

After lunch, Betta wet her comb and smoothed out the tangles in Lily's copper-red hair. She rubbed a dab of olive oil in her hands and raked it into Lilly's hair, then wove two even braids down her back. Betta wrapped the braids into a bun at the nape of Lily's neck and tied a white ribbon around it.

"I hope the sides don't spring out in this heat," said Betta, patting Lily's hair down.

"I have your hat to keep my hair down," said Lily.

Margaret handed Lily a knitted drawstring purse to carry like the young ladies do. "I made this for you. I put extra hatpins and a small comb in it." She opened the bag to show Lily. "I wish we found a pair of gloves."

"Oh Margaret, it is beautiful," said Lily, "Thank you."

Margaret hugged her sister and whispered, "I want you to know that I am sorry for being so angry and telling. And I also want you to know that I am proud of you."

Lily swallowed a sob. Her heart swelled with relief. If only Mama could say the same words or at least hug her goodbye.

Lily grabbed the paper bag with the stawberry dress, stockings, and hat.

"I'm going now, Mama," said Lily at the door. Gigi held onto Lily's waist.

"Please take me with you. I want to see you sing," cried Gigi.

Mama turned from the boiling pot.

"I can't, Gigi," said Lily. "Be good for Mama. I will tell you all about it when I get home."

"Not fair!" shouted Gigi. "Me and Violet want to go!" She stuck her thumb in her mouth and flopped on the cot next to Violet napping in the basket.

Joshua, Nelly, and Lily dodged in and out of the crowded streets to Henry Street. Lily held the paper bag close to her chest. Despite the oppressive heat and smells, Joshua's exuberance could not be contained. He ran ahead, twirled around lamp posts, skipped back to the girls, then raced up the street, again.

"Today is the happiest day of my life," exclaimed Joshua without a stutter.

Lily wished she could say the same. She should feel soaring excitement. Instead, her artist heart felt empty.

CHAPTER 42
THE LAST REHEARSAL

Wʜɪʟᴇ ᴛʜᴇ ᴄʜᴏɪʀ practiced one last time, Patty gently pressed the strawberry dress and stockings. She freshened up the flowers on the hat as well. Lily changed her clothes behind a dressing screen Patty brought down to the parlor.

Patty clasped her hands and exclaimed, "Beautiful, Lily, you look like a fine young lady." She fluffed the sleeves and patted down the sailor collar.

Miss Forsythe quickly walked in with Mr. Horowitz. Lily almost did not recognize her in a pretty flower print dress and a wide brim hat. Miss Forsythe watched Miss Lowen, plain as always, gather music sheets into a satchel.

"Martha, how do you expect to hold on to all these papers? The children know their music. Leave it."

Miss Lowen looked at her overstuffed satchel. She wore a different beige dress and a light brown hat matching her brown hair. There was not a speck of color. Lily thought Miss Lowen could easily blend into the background of any space.

"You are right," said Miss Lowen, "The children do not need the music." She tucked the satchel under her arm. "But I will take it, just in case."

Miss Wald walked into the parlor looking smart in her

cream summer suit. Her nurse's pin rested on the left lapel. She pulled out paper fans from her pocket and handed one to Lily, Nelly, Miss Forsythe, Miss Lowen, and Patty. Lily thanked Miss Wald, unfolded the paper fan with painted pink and purple flowers, and waved it in her face. A cool breeze whisked the heat off her cheeks. She folded the fan and tucked it into her knitted purse.

Miss Wald stepped back and looked at Joshua and Lily. Joshua stood as tall as he could, pulled at his suit jacket and adjusted his bow tie. He gelled and combed his brown hair into place, and his smile took up his whole face. Lily adjusted her hat and held her head up high, like a ballerina. The strawberry dress fell to her ankles and fit perfectly around her waist.

"My, my," said Miss Wald smiling, "Aren't you a delightful sight."

Lily let out a breath of relief. Mr. Horwitz stepped in next to Lily. "Why thank you, Miss Wald. I do clean up nicely don't I?" He broke out in a chuckle and winked at Lily.

Miss Wald took Lily and Joshua's hands. "I am so very proud of you two," she said, "Joshua, for bravely smoothing out the stammer and Lily dear, for taking responsibility for your errors and making amends."

"Yes, ma'am," said Lily, "But my mama is still angry. She won't come to see me sing. She hates me." Tears welled in her eyes. Mr. Horowitz stepped in and offered his handkerchief.

"Your mother loves you dearly," said Miss Wald, "She may not like your paths, but she will always love you even when you grow into an old lady."

Lily wiped her tears. Miss Wald pulled something out of her other pocket. "It seems Edith left behind a pair of gloves. I thought you might use them as part of your costume today, Lily."

The white kid gloves were soft and light. "Thank you,"

said Lily, pulling the left glove on hand and up to her elbow. "It fits!"

Mr. Horowitz brought his motor car to the front of the house. Miss Forsythe sat next to him. Lily and Joshua sat between Miss Lowen and Miss Wald. Lily felt a little queasy weaving as the car rumbled and weaved on the streets. She took deep breaths, like Mrs. Goldberg had shown her, and dabbed her forehead with Mr. Horowitz's handkerchief.

"Crazy drivers out on a holiday," said Mr. Horowitz.

"It is not a holiday if workers do not get paid," said Miss Wald, "It is a day without pay, a day the poor cannot afford."

CHAPTER 43
HILLTOP PARK

Miss Lowen and Miss Forsythe gathered around all the children at Hilltop Park. Lily watched as the crowds filed into the field entrances. Men in straw hats and ladies with parasols and wide brim hats streamed by. Lily noticed a woman nearby waving a handbill like a fan in front of her face and craning her neck in search of someone. It was Miss Smith.

"Hello, Miss Smith," said Lily, stepping close.

"Lily Taglia, is that you? Don't you look smart in your lovely dress!"

"I am with the Henry Street Settlement Children's Choir. We are singing at the game. Me and Joshua are singing a special song before the seventh inning."

"Joshua and I," corrected Miss Smith with a smile, "That is exciting news." She raised her arm toward the crowd. Soon, Mr. Reynolds was by her side. He tipped his hat toward Lily. Miss Smith relayed Lily's news.

"Big day today!," said Mr. Reynolds. "I just wired in the earlier game. Miserable. Hope the show perks up those Yankee Highlanders for a win." He hooked his arm to Miss Smith and tipped his hat again. "Remind Miss Wald I would like a statement from her, today."

Miss Forsythe led the choir to a bigroom under the stairs. A large man dressed in a tight gray striped suit and straw hat stood in the middle of the room. His belly stretched his waistcoat buttons. Below his bushy mustache, he clenched a fat cigar while talking with Miss Wald.

"That man is the one and only, Big Bill Devery, an owner of the Highlanders," whispered Mr. Horowitz, "He was once the police chief, but left as a scandal grew around him. Now he owns the Highlanders with another big shot."

"Excuse me, Mr. Devery," said Miss Forsythe, fanning her face, "Is there a window to open? The air is stuffy,"

"I assure you, little lady, that the room is satisfactory for the kiddos and you ladies," said Mr. Devery.

"It was agreed that we were to watch the game outside," said Miss Wald.

"Kids can take the heat," said Mr. Devery. He removed his straw hat and wiped his wide head, "I am not giving away paying seats to a bunch of immigrant kids on the Fourth of July."

Miss Wald took in a breath and narrowed her eyes like Margaret when she got angry. Instead of hollering, Miss Wald's remained steady and calm. "Mr. Devery, you assured me the children will watch the game, outside. They are not to be cooped up in this purgatory box."

Mr. Devery rolled his soggy cigar to the other side of his mouth and looked straight into Miss Wald's anger. "Think yourself a big boss man ordering and demanding. You ain't nothing more than a mission goody toting these ragamuffins about the city with your hand out."

Miss Wald took a step closer to the large man. How could she stand his stinking cigar? "Mr. Devery, as you can see, I am not a big boss man. I am a woman who stands for social justice against big bullies. I expect you to honor your word as you can rely on the fact that my words hold value and power in this city."

"Women like you don't scare me," said Mr. Devery. "You and my partner, Farrell, came up with this ding-bat idea. I ain't giving up seats to a bunch of straggly kids you pulled off the streets just to show off your social justice. That ain't good baseball."

The air suddenly got harder to breathe. Nelly held Lily's gloved hand.

Mr. Devery turned to the group. "Now you kiddies can wait here. Leave the door open for air circulation. You can come out at the start and sing *Star-Spangled Banner*—"

"*America the Beautiful!*" piped Miss Lowen. Her cheeks flushed red from the heat and tension.

Mr. Devery nodded to Miss Lowen, "Whatever, *America the Beautiful, Star-Spangled Banner*, all the same." He rolled his cigar in his mouth. "You march back here until the end of the 6th inning. Do your little show. I'll give ya' vouchers for lemonade and popcorn afterward."

"Hey, it's lemonade, popcorn, and a hot dog," said Mr. Horowitz. He placed his accordion next to Lily.

"No it ain't," replied Mr. Devery.

Miss Wald took in a long breath of hot cigar-infested air. She did not lose her lock on Mr. Devery. Mr. Devery smirked an ugly smile under his bushy mustache.

Lily felt sweat drip down the back of her dress and under the gloves. Sweat stains were not very lady-like. Miss Smith would not be seen with a dripping face and damp armpits.

"Excuse me, Miss Wald," said Lily, "I almost forgot. Mr. Reynolds, the newspaperman from The Sun, said he wants to get a statement from you today."

Mr. Devery's head fell from the staring standoff. "How do you know Jack Reynolds?"

Lily fought to keep her eyes on Mr. Devery. She was going to be brave. "He comes to the bakery where I bake Daily Bread. He likes Mrs. Goldberg's Knot Surprises, and he brings our teacher, Miss Smith, to the bakery and the baseball games. She likes baseball a lot."

"Jane Smith, the mayor's niece?" asked Mr. Devery.

Lily nodded. Miss Wald beamed at Lily, then turned to Mr. Horwitz.

"Mr. Horwitz, would you fetch Mr. Reynolds? Invite Miss Smith to come along as well. I am ready to make a statement. Ask him to bring his sketch pad to draw the conditions here for the paper. I am sure he would be interested in a story on how the New York Highlanders and Mr. Devery treat children —American children who love America's favorite game."

"On my way," said Mr. Horowitz, heading for the door.

"Wait! Wait!" called Mr. Devery. He threw his straw hat on the dirt floor and wiped his head again with his damp handkerchief. "You can stand behind third base. I'll get a bench out there."

"After the choir sings, the children will require lemonade, popcorn and a hotdog," said Miss Wald.

Mr. Devery picked up his hat and smacked it against his trousers. He bit down on his cigar and stormed out of the stuffy room.

CHAPTER 44
SOFTEN HEARTS

MISS FORSYTHE TOOK Miss Lowen's satchel. "The music is safe with me," she said.

Miss Lowen's complexion was back to matching her beige dress. She nodded and led the children onto the field. Shallow tufts of dirt kicked up as they made their way to the home base. Lily held onto Nellie's hand, steading the fluttery excitement building in her chest.

The teams were lined up in front of their dugouts. The Washington Nationals wore a cream-colored uniform with a large navy blue **W** on the breast pocket, navy blue stocking below the knickers, and a cream-colored cap with dark blue piping stripes and brim.

The Highlanders wore white uniforms with a large **NY** on the front of the jersey, navy blue and red striped stockings below the knickers, and a white cap with the same **NY** on the front. Lily recognized Curly Crisp with his thick eyebrows looking out from under his cap. He gave a slight wave to his neighborhood group of kids.

Lily scanned the ruckus of faces cheering in the stands and leaning against the fence bordering the field. She could not find Papa above the crowd or spy her sisters.

"They will come," she said to herself, *"They must come."*

Miss Lowen arranged the choir into three rows. Nelly took her place in the front, Joshua on the right end of the second row and Lilly in the middle of the back row. Mr. Horowitz hefted his accordion onto his shoulders.

"Not too loud," reminded Miss Lowen. "We want the voices to be heard."

Mr. Devery walked out onto the field, waving a megaphone and smiling, with the cigar stub clenched in his mouth.

The crowd quieted down. Mr. Devery took the cigar from his mouth and lifted the megaphone. "Ladies and gentlemen, boys and girls. Welcome to Hilltop Park, home of the New York Highlanders." A roar of applause and shouts erupted. Mr. Devery waved his arms again to signal attention and quiet.

"We have a Fourth of July treat for you this afternoon. Behind me stands the Henry Street Settlement Children's Choir. Don't let their ragtag look fool you, good people. These kids are genuine Americans and, I am told, sing with American heart."

Mr. Devery donned his hat to another volley of cheers and left the field. Mr. Horowitz waved his arms like Mr. Devery had done to settle the crowd. Miss Lowen knitted her eyebrows and blew a middle C into her pitch pipe. Mr. Horowitz played the introduction. The choir took in a breath.

Oh beautiful
For spacious skies,
For amber waves of grain…

Miss Lowen beamed and waved her arms, conducting the choir. The voices rose to a roar of harmony, mesmerizing the audience. People stood up and the ballplayers held their caps over their hearts. Lily spotted Curly Crisp's mop of hair fall in front of his eyes.

Lily sang strong, leading the alto section to meld with the high notes of the sopranos. When the last note faded, the field exploded in applause and cheers. Hats and small American flags waved high above the joyous crowd. Lily, overwhelmed by the grandeur, wiped a tear from her eye. She hoped Papa had heard and wished Mama wanted to be there.

The choir marched back to the stands. Family and friends grabbed their child, shouting congratulations in different languages. Joshua's mother ran her hands over her son's head, tears streaming down her cheeks.

"Angelina," called a familiar voice, "Angelina!"

Nonna plowed out of the crowd and quickly buried Nelly into her chest. Margaret ran up behind Nonna, followed by Betta, then Tony, with Gigi riding his shoulders. Lily embraced her sisters as they cheered and shouted their excitement.

"Terrific, You were all terrific," said Betta.

"We could hear you above everyone," said Margaret, hugging Llily.

"Does Mama know Gigi is here? Won't she be angry?" asked Lily.

"Hearts soften," said Betta, "Even Mama's stubborn heart."

"Is Mama here? Where's Papa?" Lily dared to hope. The two people she wanted with her on this exciting day may be at the park!

"Not sure," said Margaret. "Mr. Carter drove us with Nonna in his motor car. Papa was taking the truck."

Before Lily's disappointment could chase the joy away, Mr. Goldberg wriggled through the crowd, pulling Mrs. Goldberg behind him.

"Let through. Let through," called Mr. Goldberg as they

popped out of the crowd. Mrs. Goldberg hugged Lily, then stepped back and curtsied, low and reverent.

CHAPTER 45
REALIZED DREAMS

THE GAME BEGAN with the Highlanders on the field and the Washington Nationals batting. The sticks were wider and heavier than the broomsticks the kids played with in the alleys. Tony called them bats. The pitcher had a bigger ball and threw it faster than Lily had ever seen. All the players on the field had a leather glove on one hand.

Lily remained standing by the fence with her sisters and Tony. Nonna, Mr. Carter, and the Goldbergs found seats a few rows back.

"We come back at intermission," said Mrs. Goldberg.

"I will keep an eye out for your Papa, Lily," whispered Mr. Goldberg.

Tony spied Big John and Donny in the standing crowd. He put Gigi down, waved his arms, and called to them. Donny and John waved back.

"Mind with your sisters, Gigi," said Tony. "I'm going to the fellas."

Gigi held Margaret's hand.

"Come back when Lily sings again," said Betta.

Lily tried to follow the game. Umpires shouted, players ran and slid into bases, bats cracked and balls flew toward the furthest fences or bounced into the dust. Margaret pointed out the Christopoulos' behind the Highlanders dugout. Thea and Mr. Christopoulos stood and shouted at the players and umpire, and waved to Curly out on the field. Lily saw Mrs. Christopoulos contently knitting next to her boisterous daughter and husband.

Mr. Horowitz brought Lily a bag of popcorn, a hot dog in a long roll, and lemonade in a paper cup.

"Your payment," he said with a wink.

Lily shared the popcorn and lemonade with her sisters. They each smelled the hot dog.

"It looks like a skinny sausage," said Betta.

"Is it made from a dog?" asked Gigi.

"No," said Margaret, "I don't think so."

"I'll save it for Tony. He'll eat anything," said Lily.

The teams took turns batting the ball and playing on the field. Before the end of the sixth inning, Curly hit the ball three times. Each time he made it to a base and drove a teammate home. Lily could hear Mr. Christopoulos and Thea shout above the crowd.

Through all the excitement, Lily searched for Papa. There were a lot of tall red-headed men in caps.

Despite Curly Crisp's great batting and fielding, the Highlanders were losing 6 to 3 by the sixth inning. The heat remained thick and uncomfortable. Lily let her sisters take turns with her fan to cool their necks and faces. The inning ended, and the crowd began to thin out.

Mr. Horowitz, Miss Lowen, and Joshua met Lily at the fence. Mr. Devery motioned for them to get on the field.

"Showtime," said Mr. Horowitz. He hefted the accordion. Miss Forsythe stepped in front of him and patted his damp face with her handkerchief, then kissed him on the cheek.

"Why Miss Forsythe, people will talk," said Mr. Horowitz. Miss Forsythe winked.

Betta smoothed Lily's hair and replaced her hat with an

extra pin. Margaret tugged the strawberry dress and pulled up the white stockings. Joshua adjusted his collar and hat.

"You look like a darling child-size couple," said Betta.

"Go sing," said Gigi, shaking Lily's hand, "but tomorrow you take me to swing."

Lily searched the crowd one last time.

"It's okay," said Margaret, "We're here."

Margaret was right. Lily was surrounded by those who loved her, and she loved. Tony lifted Gigi to the back of his neck. Donny and Big John patted Joshua's shoulders. Mrs. Goldberg kissed Lily on both cheeks. Nelly held Lily's hand. Lily saw Nonna waving at her with her handkerchief. Everyone was there. Everyone, except Papa, who promised and Mama, who may have softened. Joshua offered Lily his arm. Lily smiled and the darling child-sized couple walked out to home base.

Mr. Devery shouted to the audience, holding the megaphone in one hand and a grubby cigar in the other. "Ladies and gentlemen, boys and girls! Our Yankee boys are fighting to win this game for you."

"They're a bunch of bums!" shouted a man. Agreeing jeers followed.

"No bums!" shouted a gruffer and louder voice. It was Mr. Christopoulos, "My boy, Curly Crisp, will save the day."

"Yes sir-ee," blasted Mr. Devery, "We have ourselves genuine talent with our homeboy, Curly Crisp. Raised playing stickball on the streets in the Lower East Side. But Curly and the boys need your help to boost their morale." Mr. Devery wiped his dripping face. "This better be incredible," he said to Mr. Horowitz.

"Just you wait and see," said Mr. Horowitz without losing his smile.

"Yes sir-ee, folks," shouted Mr. Devery into the megaphone. These two kiddies from the Henry Street Settlement are here to rile up that team spirit and see our boys to victory. Be sure to refresh yourselves with ice-cold beer and ice cream."

Lily and Joshua stood at home base. They saw their friends wave. Gigi was already clapping furiously. Mr. Horowitz began the introduction. Lily lifted her head to the audience. A tall redhead man waved his cap high above Big John and Gigi. Papa! But the sight that broadened Lily's smile was the short, lean woman carrying a baby in a sling. Mama jumped and waved, calling out, "Lily! Lily!"

Joshua sang out with vigor and expression.

> *Katie Casey was baseball mad*
> *Had the fever and had it bad*
> *Just to root for the home town crew*
> *Ev'ry sou*
> *Katie blew*
> *On a Saturday her young beau*
> *Called to see if she'd like to go*
> *To see a show, but Miss Kate said "No!"*
> *I'll tell you what you can do:*
> "

On cue, Lily took in a lung full of air and belted out the chorus.

> *"Take me out to the ball game,*
> *Take me out with the crowd.*
> *Buy me some peanuts and Cracker Jack,*
> *I don't care if I never get back,*
> *Let me root, root, root for the Yankees,*
> *If they don't win it's a shame.*
> *For it's one, two, three strikes, you're out,*
> *At the old ball game."*

By the last chorus, the audience swayed and sang along.

Lily and Joshua bowed and curtsied. Hats waved, cheers echoed, and the applause moved Lily to curtsy again. Finally, Lily took Joshua's arm, and the children skipped off the field.

Lily ran into Mama's waiting arms.

"You came! You came!" said Lily.

Mama wiped Lily's happy tears. "You reminded me what a special girl you are. I swallow my anger to see my daughter make me proud."

"Oh Mama," said Lily, "My dream is real with you and everyone in it."

LISTEN ~ READ ~ LEARN

REFERENCES

TAKE Me out to the Ball Game was a Tin Pan Alley song. Jack Norworth wrote the lyrics while riding a subway train and noticing a poster blaring, *Baseball Today at the Polo Grounds.* He had never attended a baseball game. Albert Von Tilzer composed the melody. The song soon became the anthem for America's baseball. Edward Meeker recorded this version in September 1908.

 https://www.youtube.com/watch?v=q4-gsdLSSQ0

America the Beautiful was originally a poem titled *Pikes Peak* by Katharine Lee Bates and published in *The Congregationalist* July 4, 1895, as *America.* Samuel Q. Ward put the poem to his composition and titled it *America the Beautiful.* Louise Homer, an international opera contralto, recorded the patriotic song in 1910 when it enjoyed "pop star" status. This version was recorded in 1924.

 https://www.youtube.com/watch?v=oQmv7FApWVE

Star Spangled Banner was written by Francis Scott Key, while witnessing the battle of Baltimore during the War of 1812. Upon seeing the American flag wave victoriously after a deafening and destructive battle, Key wrote the poem *The*

Defense of Fort M'Henry. It was published and circulated throughout the young nation, set to the music by John Stafford Smith. and re-titled *The Star Spangled Banner* in 1814. The song was played in military bands, schools and various patriotic events for over a hundred years. In 1931 *The Star Spangled Banner* earned national anthem status. The following is an Edison cylinder recording by George J. Gaskin, 1899.

https://www.youtube.com/watch?v=UyyDW_3vylI

You can find a comprehensive history of Lillian Wald and the Henry Street Settlement at https://www.henrystreet.org/about/our-history/ where highlights, the biography of Lillian Wald, the founder of Henry Street Settlement, and a video about the beginnings of public health nursing. A detailed video on the Henry Street Settlement's past, present, and future are at this site https://www.thehouseonhenrystreet.org/. Supplement your knowledge with the book **The House on Henry Street** by Lillian Wald.

The **New York Tenement Museum** has a wonderful podcast, *Our Game*, and article, *Remembering Stickball*. You can view them here: *Our Game* https://www.tenement.org/podcast-season-two-episode-1/ , and *Remembering Stickball* https://www.tenement.org/blog/remembering-stickball/ . Check out The Tenement Museum's fantastic podcast *How to be American* at https://www.tenement.org/podcast-season-1/.

The New York Yankees started their New York legacy in 1903 as the New York Highlanders. They played at Hilltop Park in the Washington Heights neighborhood of Manhattan. The newspaper reporters frequently referred to the team as the

Yankees or Yanks since they were the New York team in the American Baseball League. Find out more about the history of the New York Highlanders and New York Yankees:

https://sportsteamhistory.com/new-york-highlanders

https://stowens.medium.com/before-they-were-yankees-1f0ec52d5677

https://en.wikipedia.org/wiki/New_York_Yankees

ACKNOWLEDGMENTS

Writing a book does not happen in a vacuum. It takes sunshine, time, encouragement, faith, and love to hone the craft. There are many to thank and hug for keeping me on track and motivated. My Everyone circle expanded while I wrote this book. I can't possibly name them all, but you know who you are. Thank you, thank you.

Stephanie Larkin, Red Penguin Books publisher extraordinaire, had the right stuff, making sure I finished. She listed, delegated, and cheered on the project with genuine faith and good cheer. Thank you, Stephanie and your hard-working staff for all you do.

Beta readers played important roles in making sure the story flowed and made sense. Virtual and live gratitude go out to Meg Dedler, Melissa McMahan, Clarie Kavanaugh, and Krissy Napolitano. Advance readers who not only took the time to read an almost final version and offer their kind thoughts and words include Gary Wilson, Patricia Gold Black, Kathleen Miller Collins, and Jacqueline Goodwin. I drew an amazing amount of encouragement and wrote at full steam by participating in the writers' group. Big loving hugs go out to Eddye Lane and Christina Dankert of :55Sprint Writers and

Jacqueline Goodwin, Lale Davis and Elaine Handley for including me, the downstate member to their early morning Zoom sessions. I could not have done this project without the accountability and conversations.

I am forever grateful to the staff of the Henry Street Settlement, especially Katie Vogel, tour guide extraordinaire. Katie took the precautions and accommodated me to tour the house and ask too many questions despite the COVID 19 pandemic. Lillian Wald's work shaped New York City and the American policies we know today. Her legacy lives on in the original building on Henry Street.

Heartfelt thanks go out to my mom, Diana Truglio, who endured a terrible year since my dad's passing. She offered guidance and clarifications as the story took shape. Love you, Mom, more than words can convey.

Thank you to Penny Weber, the cover illustrator, who stealthily stepped in to re-cover The Hearts of Bakers and Artists and quickly saw and produced the vision for The Dreams of Singers and Sluggers. The beautiful depictions of the sweet faces she illustrated drew me to her.

Finally, thanks, hugs, and kisses to my husband, Matt, who endured yet another year of me writing a novel. He continues to be a thorough reader and my best cheerleader.

ABOUT THE AUTHOR

Antoinette Truglio Martin is a children's book author, memorist, and blogger. Her popular children's picture book, **Famous Seaweed Soup** was published by the Albert Whitman Company. The memoir, **Hug Everyone You Know: A Year of Community, Courage, and Cancer** (She Writes Press) chronicles her first year battling breast cancer as a wimpy patient.

Becoming America's Stories (Red Penguin Books), a Middle-Grade Historical Fiction series, debuted in 2020. The award-winning first book, **The Heart of Bakers and Artists** (formally titled **Daily Bread**), takes place in 1911 and follows nine-year-old Lily Taglia, an American-born child of Sicilian immigrants, coming of age in a crowded New York City Lower East Side tenement. The novel earned First Place in 2021 *Purple Dragonfly's Children's Book Award* in *Historical Fiction* and *Moonbeam's 2021 Children's Book Award* Gold in Pre Teen Historical Fiction. **The Dreams of Singers and Sluggers** (coming in the Fall of 2021) picks up where **The Heart of Bakers and Artists** leaves off. Lily, her family and friends reach for their dreams as new Americans. Be sure to read **Becoming America's Food Stories** where there are always good stories around good food.

Antoinette proudly holds an MFA in Creative Writing and Literature from Stony Brook/Southampton University (2016). Be sure to browse her website and blog, **Stories Served Around The Table** at https://storiesserved.com/, and read about past and present family adventures, book happenings, and life musings.

Made in the USA
Middletown, DE
21 November 2021